THE BASTARD

KING FAMILY, BOOK THREE

JULIE KRISS

The King Family Series

The Tycoon by M. O'Keefe (Book One)

The Bodyguard by S. Doyle (Book Two)

1

DYLAN

WHEN IT RAINED IN BRUJAS, Panama, it got harder to throw the drunks out. On a clear night I could toss a drunk man out of the Yaviza Bar and he'd sleep it off on the beach, listening to the water. But when it rained—thick sheets of rain, hot and heavy and nearly black—they'd fight me. They'd throw punches, or curse my mother, or—if truly shit-faced—cry. It wasn't a fun job on the best of days, but in the rain it truly sucked.

There was only one drunk I'd thrown out tonight: a man who made an ass of himself in here at least once a week. There weren't many others in the bar this evening, and it was relatively empty. I walked back to the bar, listening to the rain pounding on the roof, and took a seat on a stool. The bartender, a black-haired woman named Maqui, poured a shot of tequila and put it in front of me.

I wasn't the official bouncer at the Yaviza. That is, I wasn't on the payroll. But I was strong, I'd been in the military, and when I came here to drink I sometimes made myself useful. I got free drinks in return, along with the gratitude of the owner, the occasional offer from Maqui, and a room in the back to sleep it off on the nights I'd had too much. I could throw out the other drunks, but there was no one big enough—or dumb enough—to throw me.

I downed the shot and put the empty glass on the bar. I wasn't drunk yet, but I intended to get there. When it rained like this, the sound always kept me awake no matter where I went. The only way I'd sleep in this rain was if I drank myself into it.

What's your problem, King? Life is supposed to be perfect.

I looked around. The place was dim; with the excitement over, the remaining customers were nearly dozing off in their chairs in the steamy heat. Maqui took a rag to the bar in silence. There was nothing going on tonight. Nothing going on any night, if I was being honest. I'd left Special Ops five months ago, burned out and pushed beyond the limit of exhaustion. I didn't want to work another day, see another death. I'd packaged out, packed my single bag, and gotten on the first airplane that was taking off.

And I'd ended up here. It was supposed to be retirement in paradise, a carefree life, for once, that cost a few dollars a day. I was supposed to put my feet up, sleep with all of the local women, and drink. I'd thought I'd be relaxed for the first time in my life, finally, at age thirty-one after serving my country since I was a teenager.

I hadn't thought that I'd be...bored. Restless. Ready for something, anything, to happen.

That was the problem with living on the edge: it was hard to back away from it.

I signaled Maqui for another shot—she smiled at me, but I shook my head—and took the glass from her. The free drinks weren't really that big a deal to me, since the average drink in Brujas cost a dollar and you could eat dinner for less. The rent on my apartment cost a whopping ninety-six dollars a month, and that was for the unit that *didn't* have cockroaches. Not that it made a difference, since down here the cockroaches flew and banged against my windows. Another way to guarantee I'd never sleep.

I could always go back to the States. I could leave this hot, steamy jungle hole and take myself back to New York or San Francisco or LA, even Texas, to The King's Land ranch—my father's legacy.

Hank King had been a CEO and a real estate baron and a lot of other things, most of which made him obscenely rich. I was his son, but I was a bastard. My mother had been one of King's strings of mistresses. She'd thought she had a golden ticket when she got pregnant. Instead, Hank had dumped my mother, but he'd given me his last name on the birth certificate.

My mother had been bitter. When things didn't work out the way she wanted, she'd kept me from Hank and wouldn't give him visitation rights. Hank retaliated with lawyers; Mom retaliated by marrying a different rich man when I was two and hiring lawyers of her own. By the time I was a teenager, I was so sick of both of them and the never-ending war that was my home life, that I'd enlisted in the military and left the country.

I moved up the ranks to Special Ops. The work was hard and exhausting, and I'd felt like a shell of a human being by the end, but it kept me out of the States and away from the clutches of both my mother and my father.

Then my father had died. I hadn't gone to the funeral, hadn't answered any of his lawyer's emails about the will. I had told my sister Veronica that there was no way in hell I was coming home for the funeral. Then I'd deleted my Hotmail address, quit Spec-Ops, and come to Panama. It was dull, but no one here knew I was a King. They only knew I was American, I'd been military, I liked tequila, and I could throw a man out the door.

Works for me, I told myself. Or at least, I'd thought it would.

Sweat trickled down my temples and made my T-shirt stick to my back. I scrubbed a hand through my hair and watched as

Maqui reached up and turned on the boxy old television above the bar. Her shirt rode up as she turned the knob and one of the other guys at the bar whistled, but I looked at him and he stopped. Maqui and I weren't a steady thing, but I didn't let anyone hassle her. I knew she lived in a tiny place ten blocks away, where her mother looked after her four-year-old son while she worked. I knew she sometimes liked a no-strings fuck just like I did, and that her life was too complicated for more. Assholes at the bar were the last thing she needed.

The TV blared to life. A baseball game came on, the announcers speaking in Spanish. Maqui clicked the antique remote control and the image flipped to a soap opera, a woman weeping with smeared mascara as she shouted at a man who was leaving and slamming the door. Maqui rolled her eyes and clicked the remote again.

"—kidnapping of heiress Sabrina King—"

Maqui hit the button and the image flipped to two puppets dancing on the screen, singing in Spanish.

"Maqui," I said, my voice sharper than I intended. "Go back."

She looked at me, blinking her long dark lashes. I'd spoken in English, which I didn't usually do with her. Her English wasn't great, but it was good enough, and she caught my drift. She hit the button.

"—not clear if ransom is a motive. What we do know is that the high-profile reality star was taken from her home during an engagement party thrown for her sister—"

"Hey!" one of the men across the bar shouted in Spanish. "Put the baseball game back on again! I don't want to see this shit!"

I barely heard him. I was leaning back on my stool, my attention glued to the crappy TV screen. A female newscaster was speaking in front of a photograph of a gorgeous young woman, her dark hair cascading around her shoulders, her makeup perfect, pink gloss on her smiling lips. She seemed to be wearing a dress made of a few knots of material and not much else. She looked like a spoiled socialite, but she didn't have a socialite's blank, polite expression. Instead, she looked like the kind of girl who could tell you a rude joke and cuss you out. The picture had caught her on the edge of a laugh, as if the photographer had said something funny.

I knew that face. I knew that laugh.

Jesus. Sabrina King. My half sister.

I had three half sisters. Ronnie and Bea were from one of Hank's wives. Sabrina was from yet another mistress, one he'd married after Ronnie and Bea's mother died. Hank had been a real class act, and he didn't always use protection.

"—*disappeared from her sister's engagement party at the Texas ranch that had belonged to her late father, real estate tycoon Hank King. There were reports last month that Sabrina King ended her reality show,* Cowboy Princess, *and left Los Angeles due to threats from a stalker.*"

Someone had taken Sabrina. My littlest half sister, the one who had been sweet and overweight as a kid, then had grown into a sexy, gorgeous TV star. The half sister my military brothers teased me about relentlessly. *Hell, that's your sister? Hot damn. Can you get me her number or what?*

But we weren't close. I'd been shit to my sisters, and it wasn't their fault. Ronnie was the dutiful one, sending me updates and big news when it happened, even though my replies were always one sentence, usually sent from an ancient laptop in a barracks in a godforsaken desert somewhere while the Wi-Fi cut in and out and the guy behind me told me to hurry the fuck up. Bea was trouble, and she wasn't interested in me, so I never heard from her at all. But Sabrina was the sister who could have maybe used a big brother. A real one.

"Hey!" the man shouted again. "Turn the channel!"

"Yeah," his companion added, also in Spanish. "No one cares about this stupid American TV star. Put the baseball back on!"

I glanced at Maqui. She was watching me, her expression

unreadable. *Someone took Sabrina.* I was seeing red, and my entire world was fucking rocked—but none of these people knew it because they didn't know who I was.

Don't let on, idiot. Keep it together. I nodded at Maqui, a little stiffly maybe. "It's okay," I said, in English again. "Change the channel."

She frowned and turned back to the TV. She switched back to the baseball game, and the other men at the bar muttered happily, then began commenting on the game. No one paid any attention to me, which was what I wanted. I pushed my stool back and stood.

Maqui glanced at me. "Another?" she asked.

I shook my head. My urge to get drunk was gone. Sabrina had been abducted straight from the goddamned ranch, where she should have been secure. Where the hell was her security detail? What about the cameras and the electronic alarms? Had she taken any personal belongings? Had they seen anyone strange hanging around the ranch lately?

The questions tumbled through my mind, each on the heels of the other. Because I'd had a specialty in Special Ops: kidnappings. The high-profile ones that came with ransom demands. I was skilled in getting people out of those situations—without bloodshed, if possible, but if it wasn't possible—well, I had training and skills, and I knew how to use them.

Skills I could use to find Sabrina right now, if I was in the middle of the action instead of sitting in this hellhole.

I had to get out of here, now.

I'd been here for months, but it would take me fifteen minutes at most to clear out. Pack my single bag, leave a note in Spanish for my landlord along with a few dollars. There was no one here to even say goodbye to.

It was seven hours' drive to the nearest airport, over roads that were sketchy at best. The rain wouldn't help. Still, I'd get there as fast as I could. If I wasn't already too late and Sabrina wasn't already dead.

If I wanted excitement, it looked like I was about to get it.

I turned to the door and glanced at Maqui one last time, to say something—what, I had no idea. Not goodbye, because we'd never been anything to each other in the first place except a few casual fucks. We had always been clear on that. But she was still watching me, and her expression had gone stony.

"She is very pretty, yes?" she said to me in English.

Sabrina. She was talking about Sabrina. "It isn't what you think," I said.

Maqui shrugged, her expression still hard. Whether she followed what I'd said, or simply didn't care, I couldn't tell. "You know this pretty girl, Sabrina King," she said. "You're leaving for her."

The men who came to the Yaviza Bar liked to make passes at Maqui. They all wanted to get into her bed. I was the only man she'd said yes to—in fact, it had been her idea. She had made me an offer one night, and I hadn't said no. It was an offer she hadn't made anyone else since her child's father left.

If she was attached, then that was too bad, because whatever we had was done. But she had the wrong idea about why.

I hesitated, the words on the tip of my tongue: *she's my sister.* But the King family was too famous, too prominent, and far too rich. It would be all over town in seconds. I couldn't admit to her that I was one of them. The instinct, even after all these years, was always to protect the family. The name. The privacy. At any cost.

So I settled for an explanation that wasn't one. "She isn't mine."

Maqui picked up a glass from the bar and turned away. "Goodbye, Dylan."

Well, I fucked that up. I should have played it differently, somehow, though I was damned if I could see how. In the meantime, someone could be hurting Sabrina with every second that passed. I turned and walked out the door.

It was time to go home after all these years. Time to be useful for the first time in forever. Time to be, however reluctantly, a King.

I was going back. And there was nothing anyone could do to stop me.

2

MADISON

"You have got to be kidding me," I said into the phone. The woman ahead of me in the Starbucks line glanced back over her shoulder, giving me a glare. I pushed my sunglasses up onto my head and glared back.

"I'm not kidding," said my investigator, Max, on the other end of the line. "My source in Brujas says Dylan King has left town. Apparently he saw something on the news about Sabrina's kidnapping and he walked out the door."

"Right," I said. "And who exactly is your source in that backwater place?"

"Maddy, you know that's confidential."

"Which means it's a woman," I said. "Is she pretty, at least?"

"What do you care? The information is good."

"Shit." I had only landed in LA a few hours ago. I'd flown to Texas for Ronnie King and Clayton Rorick's engagement party— at which Ronnie's sister Sabrina had been kidnapped by a crazy stalker. Sabrina had been tracked down pretty quickly by Garrett Pine, who was the sheriff and Sabrina's maybe-boyfriend, and she hadn't been seriously hurt, but it had been a crazy night all the same. I'd spent part of the next day helping deal with the press and the local cops, and then I'd flown back to California. As a partner at my firm I couldn't stay in Texas, kidnapping or no kidnapping.

So with Sabrina safe and everything on the mend, I'd come back to LA. But I was exhausted. I needed caffeine more than anything, and then I needed to get to work. And this line wasn't moving.

"I take it Dylan doesn't know Sabrina is safe," I said to Max.

"Probably not," he replied. "That news report that leaked out before Sabrina was found went viral. There was an update by this morning, but if Dylan was already on the road, he wouldn't have seen it."

"Do we know for sure that he's coming back for her, and he isn't headed somewhere else?"

"Since he bought a ticket for a flight to Dallas that took off ten minutes ago, my guess is yes, we're sure," Max said.

Damn, he really was a good investigator, even though he was pushing seventy. Worth every penny. I tapped my spiked heel, thinking. If Dylan was coming back, this was big news for the King family—my clients. Very, very big. "What else do we know?"

"He paid for the ticket with cash and he didn't check a bag."

Which meant that either Dylan didn't think he'd be in the States long, or he didn't have any belongings to pack. My guess was option two.

Dylan King had spent his adult life in military barracks or on assignment. He'd quit Special Ops over five months ago, but he was still living out of a bag. A fact I knew because of Max and his informant, whoever she was.

"It makes no sense," I said to Max as the Starbucks line

moved up a painfully slow step. "After all these years, he thinks he's going to suddenly play hero?"

"He doesn't have to play hero at all," Max pointed out. "Twelve years in Special Ops makes him bona fide. As for why he's coming now, we know he specialized in kidnapping cases. Maybe he feels he can help out."

"And he's going to find out it's already over." The woman ahead in line glared at me again, and I moved the phone away from my mouth. "It's business, bitch," I told her. "Deal with it."

"Asshole," she said, and my respect for her actually went up a notch. At least she wasn't a pushover.

"If he wasted a flight, that's too bad," Max said. "If he hadn't gone so far off the grid, at least he'd know what was going on. It's impossible to keep tabs on this guy in the middle of the jungle."

It was true. I had one Hotmail address for Dylan, and that was all. When I'd used it to inform him his father had died and he needed to come to the States to discuss the will, I had gotten a one-line response: *Not going to happen. Give up and fuck off.*

Then Dylan had deleted the email account entirely and vanished into Panama.

The King family, you could say, was a little dysfunctional.

I actually sort of liked Dylan's half sisters. Veronica, known as Ronnie, was smart and responsible. She was about to marry Clayton Rorick after an epic romance that spanned years of angst and unrequited love. That kind of romance wasn't for me, but I was glad she was happy. Sabrina, the youngest, looked like an LA type, but underneath she was sweet and actually rather charming. She, too, was in love, with the sheriff who had saved her from her stalker. They were an unlikely couple, but he seemed pretty smitten. It was too early for me to talk to her about a prenup— I'm a lawyer, it's my nature—but at least I knew she was in good hands.

Bea, the middle sister, was tougher. Her debts had gotten her into trouble, which meant she needed money from her father's estate. But I had a feeling that Bea could turn things around—that is, if she actually wanted to.

So the sisters were at least trying, sort of, to have a real relationship. It would be easier now that their father was dead. I worked for Hank for years, and I owed him a great deal, but even I could easily see that he was an epic asshole who'd treated his daughters like less than nothing. It had always been Dylan, the one and only son, who had interested Hank.

To be honest, Dylan interested me, too.

Alongside his legal affairs, Hank King had hired the firm to keep detailed tabs on his son and report regularly. Hank hated that Dylan wasn't under his thumb. In all his years of marrying and cheating, Hank had never had another son—only Dylan. Even in his absence, Dylan had been Hank's favorite child, the one whose bitch of a mother had kept him away, the one Hank always hoped would come back and take over the family business. He'd neglected his daughters without a shred of guilt, but he'd torn himself to pieces over Dylan. So I'd hired Max and a few other investigators over the years, and I'd kept a file. And I'd been paid for it.

I might not have Dylan's email address anymore, but I knew everything else it was possible to know. Even though I'd never met the man in person.

Then Hank had suddenly died, and I was still keeping tabs on Dylan. Because I was Hank's lawyer and the estate was my business.

Which meant Dylan King was my business.

I even knew who Dylan had slept with over the years. That part wasn't really my business. That was more of a hobby, let's say.

"Okay, so we don't tell him," I said to Max. "Let him come home and I'll catch him in Texas and break the news to him. I'll get on a flight back to Dallas." God, even the thought was exhausting. But if the prodigal son was coming home, then I would have to meet him. I had no other way of talking to him except tackling him face-to-face. If he had a phone number, I'd certainly had never had it.

Max was saying something about Dallas. "Sorry, I missed that. What?"

"I was saying you don't need to go to Dallas," Max said. "Dylan King is coming to you."

"What does that mean?"

"It means he flies to LA first and changes airlines. He has a layover. He'll be at LAX in six hours."

I looked out the window at the golden sunshine, the glint of lights off the cars of LA traffic outside the Starbucks window. Hank King's main holdings were in Texas, but my firm was based in LA, where Hank had a penthouse. Dylan, the man I knew only through a file—and phone call reports like this one—was going to be here. Here. In six hours.

My heart sped up and my knees went a little weak. For a second, I couldn't think of anything to say. I'd hit the top of my profession by age thirty, I'd made damned close to seven figures last year, and I'd worked for the most difficult man in Texas. I'd served people papers that made them cry, sat in conference rooms and watched people's lives fall apart without feeling a thing. My staff called me the Ice Princess behind my back. And now my knees were weak at the thought of one man I'd never met landing at LAX.

I was never weak. *Never.*

"Miss," the girl behind the Starbucks counter said. "Can I take your order?"

I stared at her. "What?"

"Your order," the girl said. The woman in front of me had already ordered and stepped aside, and she gave me a curious look. The man in line behind me did, too.

"I don't..." I couldn't think. My brain was a blank except for the words *Dylan King is going to be here in six hours. After all this time.*

"Maddy?" Max said through the phone.

Dylan King is going to be here in six hours.

"I'll call you back," I said to Max. I ended the call and walked away from the counter, heading for the door. I pushed out onto the Beverly Hills street and put my sunglasses on, staring at nothing as people brushed past me.

Dylan King. I could see his face clearly in my mind, because my file had a collection of photographs. Dylan in high school, Dylan in basic training. Dylan on the beach in Panama, walking shirtless through the sand, a pensive look on his face. Dylan in front of a bank in Panama City after withdrawing some of his military pay.

He'd grown out his hair since leaving the forces, and its dark strands were longer now on his forehead and behind his ears. He'd also grown a beard, which was dark and trim against his perfect jaw. His time in Central America had made him look a little disreputable but he still had that trained intensity, a bad boy with well-honed steely strength and grace. He looked like a man who would break your neck as soon as that pesky hangover cleared up.

And, yeah, it was my job as his father's lawyer to investigate him. But I'd spent a *lot* of time off the clock looking at that file. At those photographs.

Some of the photos had women in them. Even while deployed, Dylan King had found women around the globe. There was an ambassador's daughter in Beirut who had been only twenty-two and looked like a lingerie model. There was a curvaceous government aide in Chechnya who had sent him a string of filthily erotic emails we'd intercepted. He'd only been in Morocco for nineteen days for an assignment, but we still got a picture of him with a sensationally beautiful woman in one of Marrakesh's most expensive hotels, sipping a cup of mint tea as she played footsie with him under the table. I had spent way too much time in my off hours looking at those pictures, rereading those dirty emails—good God, what those two had gotten up to—and wondering if there was a country on the planet Dylan King hadn't yet conquered in the sack.

He's going to be here in six hours, Maddy. What are you going to do?

I took a breath. I was a professional, and I had a job to do. Hank had always wanted his son, his one and only son, to come back to the States and stay. He'd never been able to achieve it; Dylan had always shut his father down, when he bothered to answer his emails at all. Now Hank was dead, but Sabrina getting kidnapped had achieved what Hank had never been able to do. In six hours I had my one and only shot at getting Dylan King back in the fold.

And if the thought of coming face-to-face with Dylan made my blood pound, which never happened, I could deal with that.

I pulled out my keys and headed for the parking lot and my car. Dylan King was in for the surprise of a lifetime, and he wasn't going back to the jungle. When he heard what I had to tell him, he'd be home for good.

3

DYLAN

EIGHT HOURS DRIVING through the jungle—a mudslide on the road made things interesting—and another three waiting at the airport for the next available flight to go out. Six hours in the air, and I still wasn't back in Texas. I was in LA, of all places, where already people were looking at me like I didn't belong. Maybe it was the tat on my arm or the untrimmed beard. Maybe it was the old jeans and T-shirt I was wearing—literally the clothes I'd had on my back when I'd seen the news story in the Yaviza Bar. Maybe it was the fact that I smelled, which I definitely did. Maybe it was just my scowl as I thought about Sabrina. Whatever the reason, people gave me a wide, wary berth as I shouldered my single leather bag and walked through the crowds in LAX.

I pulled out my cell phone and turned it on. I had a four-hour layover before I got on a plane to Dallas, and I needed to find out what was happening with Sabrina. I needed to reach whoever was in charge and offer them my services—if Sabrina was still alive. *Welcome back to America,* I told myself as I configured the signal. *Do you know what year it is?* I had a feeling I was going to need more than a dollar to buy a beer.

Four hours. I could use four hours. I had no email—fuck email—but at least I had a phone, though no one but my old commanding officer had the number. I could start assessing the situation by phone, coordinate a plan. I was exhausted, but I'd gone longer than this without sleep before. All I needed was somewhere quiet.

I was still looking down at the phone when a pair of women's legs approached me. A long, elegant pair of women's legs, feet in open-toed heels. They stopped in front of me and a voice said, "Dylan King."

It wasn't a question. I racked my brain quickly, trying to remember if I had any exes who had moved to LA. I couldn't think of any. I fixed my gaze to the legs and let it slide upward.

She was almost as tall as me. A killer body, those long legs attached to a firm pair of hips, a narrow waist, a nice set of breasts. All of it clothed in a short dress made of some kind of expensive cream-colored linen that fit her like a glove. Her honey-brown hair was long and tied back in a low ponytail; a set of bangs swept over her forehead. A pair of sunglasses was pushed up on her head. She had brown eyes rimmed with dark lashes, a straight nose, and lips that were pink and glossy. She looked like a wet dream, perfect and unattainable.

"Who the hell are you?" I said.

The woman looked me up and down, her expression giving nothing away. "Madison White," she said. "I'm your father's lawyer."

This was my father's lawyer? I searched my brain for the name and remembered the emails I'd received after Hank died. The last email was to tell me something about Hank's will, and I'd replied something along the lines of *fuck off* right before I hit Delete on the entire account. Then I'd had a letter from her firm, sent to my former unit. It was an offer from Clayton Rorick, saying he was going to marry my half sister Ronnie and offering me two and a half million dollars to stay away from King Industries.

I'd mailed the letter straight back to Ronnie and told her not to marry that dirtbag. But since Sabrina had been kidnapped at Ronnie's engagement party, I was guessing the message didn't take.

I'd pictured a gray-haired battle-ax on the other side of those emails and letters, not this wickedly sexy female. Though I shouldn't have been surprised. Hank always had a weakness for beautiful women.

There was a more important problem, though. "How the fuck did you know I was here?" I asked her.

Her lips pressed together in a firm line. "I have my sources of information, Mr. King. You and I need to talk."

"Sure we do," I said. "We need to talk about how you knew what flight I was on, considering I only bought the ticket hours ago. For cash."

The corner of her mouth turned up. She might look like a fantasy—albeit a buttoned-up one—but that smirk and the look in those dark eyes said she was a woman who was used to winning. "Mr. King," she said, "I worked for your father for four years before he died. Do you honestly think he didn't know where you were and what you were doing?"

"I don't give a shit what my father knew," I said, though silently I wondered who had leaked information, because last I checked I didn't have a GPS up my ass. "And if you're so well-informed, then you know my sister Sabrina has been kidnapped. So I'm on my way to Dallas." I brushed past her—she smelled good, clean with a whiff of some kind of perfumey shampoo, giving my body a brief twinge of regret that we weren't both naked—and continued through the crowd in the terminal, heading to check in for my next flight.

"Wait," I heard her call after me. I didn't stop, just kept walking, shoving my phone in my pocket. Miss Legal Wet Dream would have had to buy a ticket to get this far into the airport. She'd wasted her money. She could get back in her no doubt expensive car and leave me the hell alone.

But she didn't. I heard her heels clicking behind me, jogging surprisingly fast. "Wait," she said again, and her hand reached out and grabbed my arm.

I turned. She'd grabbed my biceps, and her touch burned into my skin beneath the sleeve of my T-shirt. She looked a little frazzled, as if she hadn't quite expected me to walk away. As if she hadn't wanted me to.

Then she got control again, and her chin went up, her eyes going hard. "You don't understand, Mr. King," she said. "We really do need to talk."

"We don't," I said. "And Mr. King was my father. My name is Dylan."

She blinked those dark lashes, and for a split second there was uncertainty in her eyes. I realized she hadn't dropped her hand, and it was still on my biceps. I glanced down at it. Her fingers were long and elegant, her skin pale against my tan. She wore a gold ring studded with small, understated stones on her middle finger, feminine and expensive, and she had a narrow gold designer watch on her wrist. Looking at her white skin, her expensive jewelry against my tats and worn T-shirt, made my blood thump hard in my veins for a heady second, sending a shot straight down below my belt.

I don't have a type. I like women—beautiful women, available women, women with no strings attached. I like women who flirt and lick their lips when they look at me, women who like to fuck. I like women who know the drill: we fuck, it's spectacular, we both get off, repeat as many times as needed. Then we move on. It's animal instinct, pure and simple.

So high-class women weren't specifically my type. But the sight of Madison White's hand on my skin made my head spin, and for a second I forgot where I was. Every part of me woke up.

I looked back up at her face and saw that her lips had parted, as if she was as surprised as I was. Then she dropped her hand and stepped back, as if trying to lessen the effect. "Your half sister is fine," she said in a rush. "They found her last night, shortly after she was kidnapped. They caught the guy. She's unharmed. It's over."

I stared at her hard, wondering if she had a reason to lie. "Sabrina wasn't hurt?" I asked.

Madison White shook her head. "No. I swear it. You can look it up yourself—it's all over the news. She's fine."

I blew out a breath, ran a hand over my face, rasped it over my beard. "Fuck," I said. Relief hit me like a blow, followed quickly by tiredness so heavy it threatened to make my shoulders droop. "They took him down? The man who abducted her?"

"Yes."

Without me. So much for Dylan King, superhero. "What did he want? Why did he take her?"

Madison blinked. "He's nuts, apparently. He went to high school with Sabrina and has been obsessed with her ever since. He thinks he's in love with her. Sometimes women in the public eye, like Sabrina, attract creeps."

"She isn't just any woman. She's my sister."

That smirk again. "Half sister. One you haven't seen in years."

"Yeah? And how do you know that?"

"Well, I could be a genius. Or maybe I know it because Sabrina told me. I just got back from The King's Land last night."

That gave me a punch in the gut, which surprised me. The thought of Madison at my family home, talking to my sister, learning things about her that I didn't know, made me strangely jealous. Which I shouldn't be, because this woman was one hundred per cent right. I hadn't seen Sabrina in years. Ronnie or Bea, either. I'd been a crack Special Ops agent and an excellent fighter, but I was a terrible brother. A terrible son. It was pure survival instinct, the drive to get the fuck away from anything King. I didn't like to think about my reasons.

Except now, after all these years, I was fucking thinking about it.

"Okay," I said to Madison. "I still have no idea how you found me, but thank you for the update. It's good news. I'm still going to see Sabrina. I'm off to take a nap, then get on a plane to Dallas."

"Wait," she called as I turned to go.

I looked back at her, still walking. "What?"

"You're not going to Dallas."

"Sorry, but I am."

Madison crossed her arms. "You're not, actually. But please, don't take my word for it. Just go to the counter and try to check in."

I shook my head, turned away, and kept walking.

And twenty minutes later I was fucking steamed.

I'd *had* a ticket to Dallas when I left Panama. Bought and paid for. I had to switch airlines, though which meant at the low-tech ticket counter in Panama it had been two separate tickets. The problem was, when I got to the second airline's counter, I found my ticket had been canceled.

Completely canceled, no exchanges and no refunds. And even if the flight hadn't been full—which it was—I didn't have enough money to buy a new ticket on the spot. I could try to get on the next flight to Dallas, but it didn't leave until morning.

I thanked the woman behind the counter before I left, because it wasn't her I was mad at. I had a pretty good idea who was to blame.

Sure enough, she was still standing where I'd left her, though she had moved to the side to let the crowds walk by. She was talking on her cell phone, her weight leaning on one hip, her head tilted. How the hell old was she? Thirty maybe, yet she was my father's lawyer, dealing with his multimillion-dollar estate. In the seconds before she noticed my approach I heard her say into the phone, "No, Gerald. Tomorrow isn't good enough. I need that paperwork filed today. Go to the courthouse if you have to. Yes, I know it's getting late and the traffic is bad. Figure it out."

She caught sight of me from the corner of her eye and turned my way. She was obviously expecting my return, which was why she hadn't left. I strode toward her, and I was sure I looked dangerous, but the only sign she'd noticed was a brief widening of her chocolate-brown eyes. "I have to go," she said into the phone and hung up.

"No flight, huh?" I said when I got close.

"I warned you," she said. "Honestly, Mr. King, if you hadn't deleted your email address, or if anyone had the number to that phone you're carrying, I wouldn't have to resort to these measures. Next time you should listen to me."

"Or maybe you should listen to me." I kept coming, closer and closer, until I was in her space. "I don't know what you're up to, but I don't like anyone interfering with my plans."

I'd interrogated terrorists who looked at least a little bit disconcerted when I talked like this, but Madison White's only sign of weakness was that she licked her glossy bottom lip. "Your plans to go back to Dusty Creek, Texas?" she asked. "What were you going to do there now that you're not needed? Go sit at The Bar and guzzle Southern Star?"

So she'd been to Dusty Creek. She'd talked to my sisters. She'd been to The King's Land, the estate I hadn't visited in years. In fact, if I somehow got on my flight, did the drive from Dallas, and got to The King's Land, I wasn't even sure anyone would let me in. And I sure as hell didn't have a key.

I couldn't let on that she was even a little bit right, so I said, "What do you want with me?"

She sighed, as if I was the one trying her patience. "I told you, we have to talk. There are things you need to know about the will. About your sisters and the rest of the family. You would know this if you'd responded to my email with something other than the F-word. Or if you'd responded at all to the registered letter I sent to your unit, which was your last known address."

I shook my head. My commanding officer had forwarded that letter on, and I'd thrown it away unopened. The one from Clayton Rorick, though—that one I'd opened. "I don't want any of Hank's money."

"If it was just about money, do you think I'd go to all this trouble?" For the first time her voice sharpened, and I caught a glimpse of the feisty bitch she probably was in the courtroom. It really, really shouldn't have turned me on. Damn it. "Listen to me, Dylan King. No one has been able to drag you out of the jungle. *No one.* I've been waiting for you to come back to the States ever since your father died, and not because I need something to fill my time. I canceled your flight. I came all the way to LAX. I paid money for a ticket I'm not going to use. I'm standing in this depressing terminal in my six-hundred-dollar heels, and it isn't because I need a hobby. Get it through your self-obsessed head. *This is fucking important.*"

I felt my eyebrows go up. I should have been pissed off. Instead, my blood got a little hotter.

It turned out I had a type, after all.

"You terrify a lot of men with speeches like that?" I asked her, challenging her. "Make their balls shrivel up?"

"All the time," she said, her gaze never wavering from mine. "And if they don't shrivel, I bust them. It's what I do."

"You gonna bust mine?"

"If I have to."

My balls had other ideas when it came to her, but I shut them up for once. Right now I looked like I'd rolled out of the garbage pit behind the Yaviza Bar, and I probably smelled like it, too. I had known a lot of women, and I knew when a woman wasn't going to sleep with me. The way I looked and smelled right now, this woman wouldn't touch me with a ten-foot pole.

But there had been that zing of energy when she'd touched me. I was familiar with that, too, though I'd never felt it nearly so strong.

Maybe getting my balls busted by Madison White wouldn't be so bad.

Aside from the long shot of getting her into bed, Madison interested me. She was a woman who had guts and obvious brains. When was the last time I'd had a woman challenge me? I couldn't even remember. It had been a very, very long time.

And I couldn't get to know her better if I was on a lonely flight to Dallas, with nothing at the other end.

"All right," I said, shouldering my bag. "You win. I'm all yours." She blinked, and for a second I thought her pupils went wide, but maybe I imagined it. I still gave her a grin. "Do with me what you will, Madison White. Lead the way."

4

MADISON

IT WORKED.

I mean, of course it worked—I'd backed Dylan King into a corner with nowhere else to go. But still, with a man like Dylan, you never quite knew what he was going to do. He'd been in Special Ops, dealing with some of the most dangerous and violent people on the planet. He had skills that would probably give me nightmares. Corralling him at LAX with a canceled flight was a little bit like corralling a tiger and hoping it started to purr instead of ripping your throat out.

But my tiger followed silently at my heels as I led him out of the terminal and to the garage where I'd parked my car. He didn't walk next to me and he didn't try to lead. He didn't argue and he'd stopped protesting. It was, in an unsettling way, exactly like leading a tiger on a leash, listening to the soft pads of its huge paws as it walked behind you.

It gave me chills up my spine. And beneath my expensive dress, it turned me on.

Don't be an idiot, Maddy.

I would *not* be sleeping with Dylan King. That was a given. The reasons were many. I never slept with clients; I never slept with men I couldn't control. I didn't have sex very often, and I didn't do relationships. I wasn't some sappy girl waiting for her white lace wedding day. I already knew that happy-ever-afters didn't exist.

I knew that people saw me as cold, and maybe they were right, but the truth was I liked orgasms. A lot. It was just that I had my hand and a careful selection of vibrators, and I could have as many orgasms as I wanted without all of the pesky inter-personal stuff or the risky body fluids. Frankly, it worked for me.

"Where are we going, by the way?" Dylan asked behind my shoulder. "In case you were willing to tell me." The drawl of his voice worked slowly and warmly up my spine. I hated to admit it, but his voice alone was better than the most expensive vibrator in my secret drawer. Damn it. Now I had a voice to go with the photos I'd been looking at for years. I practically had to press my knees together.

"The Hexagon Hotel," I answered him, pressing my key fob and clicking open my Porsche. "I booked you a suite there."

"That's awfully nice of you, considering you had no idea I'd actually use it."

"I had a hunch," I said, opening the driver's door and getting behind the wheel.

Dylan got in the passenger side, putting his single bag on his lap. He should have looked entirely out of place, a vagrant straight from the jungle on my expensive leather seats, but he didn't look out of place at all. Dylan King looked in command of every situation, even when he was being driven around LA in a car that practically made him fold his legs to his chin. Instead of looking ridiculous, he looked like he could take out a hostage situation with his pinky finger. I pointedly ignored how hot he was and started the car.

"The Hexagon is expensive," Dylan said as we pulled out of the lot. "Why do I get the feeling you're not being generous?"

"Because I'm not," I told him, putting on my sunglasses. "The suite is billed back to the King estate. So, in fact, you're paying every penny."

"My sisters are, you mean," he said, looking out the window at the freeway going by.

"That's one of the things we need to talk about."

"So talk," he said.

"I'll wait until we're at the hotel." I'd had these conversations before, and it wasn't best to do them while I was trying to concentrate on highway traffic. "Tell me about what you've been doing since you left the military."

There was a pause, long enough for him to let me know he was choosing to go along with the change of topic, for whatever reasons of his own. "Do you care?" he asked.

He had no idea how much I cared about the details of his life. How many of them I knew. "Your father always wanted you to come back and take over the business. He could never figure out why you didn't."

"Maybe it was because he was here," Dylan said. "The entire country wasn't big enough to hold me and him and my mother, as far as I'm concerned."

I could understand that. Dylan's mother was one of Hank's five-minute mistresses, and by the time their affair was done, she and Hank had hated each other. There had been a bitter custody battle when Dylan was young. He'd probably had more than enough of both of them.

I knew what it felt like to want more than a continent between you and your parents. But that was my business.

"Even after Hank died, you stayed away," I said. "Why? What was so great about Panama?"

He didn't catch the subtext of my question: *Who was she?*

"I was taking a vacation," Dylan said. "It was pretty fucking relaxing. You should try it sometime."

He hadn't looked relaxed in any of the pictures I'd seen. He'd looked debauched, sure, but he'd also looked coiled with tension. Then again, in every photo I had of him, that was how Dylan King always looked. It was how he looked now.

Still, I couldn't exactly tell him I didn't believe him because of my file of photos, could I?

"It must have been a nice vacation after all those years in the military," I said.

Dylan replied by changing the subject. "How did you come to work for my father?"

That was easy. "He was a client of my boss, Jack Stoneman," I said. "Jack was his lawyer for years."

"And he isn't your boss anymore?"

"Jack is dead, actually," I said. "By the time he died, I was close to becoming a partner in the firm. He passed the King file to me and made me partner before his last illness. Hank took to me and didn't fire the firm, so I've worked the file ever since."

"So Jack Stoneman and then my father," Dylan observed. "You seem to have a way with powerful old men."

My defenses went up and my back went tight. I glared at him. "Is that an insinuation?"

He gave me half a grin. "No, it isn't. I don't think you slept your way to the top. Though if you did, it isn't my business. I'm just saying that powerful assholes don't intimidate you."

"How did you know Jack was an asshole?" Hank was a given.

"All rich, powerful men are assholes. That's how they stay rich and powerful."

I turned back to the road. For a second I couldn't say anything. How many times in my career had I been accused of fucking my bosses, my clients? Too many, either in outright digs or murmured accusations. The jokes behind my back were probably even worse. No one could believe that I was good at my job. It was true, I had a way of handling powerful men like Jack and Hank—I knew how to look them in the eye and give as good as I got, just like a man would. It made them respect me. The fact that I was good-looking and liked to dress to show off my assets made everyone think they knew things they didn't.

But Dylan didn't think like everyone else. I'd met him half an hour ago, and he'd figured me out right away.

"I wasn't," I told him. "Sleeping with them, that is." Shit, I could kick myself. I didn't need to explain myself to Dylan King, or to anyone. "I got where I am because I'm an excellent lawyer. No other reason."

Dylan shook his head. "My commanding officer in SO was a fifty-year-old man who had done six tours of duty," he said. "He had burn scars on his arms he didn't talk about. He was two hundred and fifty pounds of pure muscle. He could make new recruits cry. I've seen him stay awake for forty-eight straight hours. And you somehow got me into this car faster than he could have. If he'd waylaid me at the airport, we'd still be arguing."

I tried not to feel flattered, even though I was. "Simple," I said. "You agreed because you want to have sex with me, and part of you thinks that by agreeing you're improving your chances."

That made him laugh, which sent a shiver down my spine. "So you're not above using sex to get what you want."

"The promise of sex. Not the delivery of it."

"Duly noted."

"I mean it," I said, gripping the wheel and hoping I sounded icy cool. "I suppose we should clear the air right away. I won't sleep with you. I don't mix sex with business. Even if I wanted to, which in this case, I do not."

Liar, liar, I thought.

"Fine," he said. "I'll make a note." He didn't sound angry. He didn't even sound concerned. He just looked out the window again. Something told me this wasn't over.

Something told me it was only beginning.

5

DYLAN

I HADN'T BEEN to the Hexagon before, but everyone knew the name. It was one of those hotels where you could see an A-list movie star sitting in one of the lounges, being interviewed for *Rolling Stone*. They'd keep talking and you'd just walk on by, because at the Hexagon that wasn't an unusual occurrence.

It worked for me. Celebrities bored me stupid, and I hadn't seen a movie in years. The desk clerk only gave me a slightly surprised look, taking in my less-than-formal attire as I checked in. At first I assumed he didn't question me because I was with Madison. Then I realized that even as I was, I was probably dressed better than Johnny Depp after a bender.

Madison hadn't lied—she'd booked a penthouse suite. It was huge, it was immaculate, it was quiet, and it probably cost someone's salary, but at the moment I didn't care. The minute I was through the door I kicked off my shoes and pulled my T-shirt over my head.

"What are you doing?" Madison asked, alarmed.

"Taking a shower," I said, my hands dropping to my belt buckle.

She pointed to herself with one manicured nail. "I'm standing right here."

"So leave," I said, hooking my thumb over the waist of my jeans and boxer briefs and pushing it all down. "I'm not waiting."

"Jesus." She whirled, putting her back to me so fast it made her hair swirl. "What did I just tell you about sex and business?"

"This isn't sex, it's nudity," I said. "Nudity is our natural state, Maddy. You were born that way. I assume you *were* born, and not created by Zeus on a particularly bad day."

"Bite me," she said, her composure returned. "Don't call me Maddy. And go take a shower. You reek."

I padded away from her turned back and headed for the shower. I really was rank. "Feel free to search my things," I said over my shoulder. "You'll probably find it interesting."

I took more time than my usual thirty seconds in the shower, scrubbing myself clean. It felt good to wash the jungle off me. The old injury in my right shoulder was acting up, sending pain down the center of my back. My right knee was aching, and the scar tissue on the side of my neck felt tight. At thirty-one, I felt the effects of the road I'd been traveling. My left middle finger didn't sit straight—it had been broken twice—and my head throbbed with exhaustion, but otherwise I was in one piece. I'd survived twelve years in SpecOps without losing a body part or losing my life. I called that a goddamned achievement.

After months of boredom masquerading as relaxation, I was ready for action.

I turned off the shower and wrapped a towel around my waist. When I came back out, Maddy—yeah, I was going to call her that —was sitting on the penthouse sofa, a drink in front of her. She had her usual perfect composure.

"You're still here," I observed.

"Was I supposed to go somewhere?" she asked.

"I thought maybe you'd run away."

"Because you took your clothes off?" She rolled her eyes. "Don't flatter yourself."

I felt myself grinning at her. "Men strip for you all the time, do they?"

"Only when I tell them to."

I had picked up my bag, but I paused and looked at her. "You know what that was, right? Flirting. You just flirted with me."

She looked surprised for a second. Then she said, "I told you —the promise of sex, not the delivery. It was a persuasion tactic. Don't get the wrong idea. And do *not* take that towel off."

"The lady protests too much," I said, but I spared her this time. I pulled clothes from my bag and retreated to the bathroom to change.

I wasn't really sure why I had stripped in front of her. I didn't usually act like that. It had been an impulse, a desire to see if I could push her buttons, make her react. And, I'll be honest, part of me wanted her to see the goods, as it were. Just in case she was interested.

In my experience, most women were interested. But of course Maddy White had to be different.

She hadn't taken the bait. But she also hadn't called security or the police, and she hadn't kicked me in my exposed nuts. I'd have to take it and call it a win.

I put on my clothes—dark green cargo pants, navy blue T-shirt. I brushed my teeth. My hair and beard could use a trim, but otherwise I looked almost American again. I came back into the main room and found Maddy pouring me a drink, which she handed to me without asking. "Sit," she said, all business now.

I took the drink and sat on the couch. I looked into my glass and saw that it was whiskey, which was my favorite drink. A lucky guess, obviously. I tilted my head back and downed it.

Maddy took a seat on the sofa across from me. "Here it is," she said in her blunt way. No lawyer-speak, which I admired. "Your father died, and you're in his will. In a roundabout way."

I put my glass down and waited.

"Hank always wanted you to come back and take over the family business," Maddy said. "But when you didn't, he hired a man named Clayton Rorick, initially to help him manage his investments. Hank and Clayton became close—"

"I know Clayton," I said. "He's the asshole who offered me money to stay away."

"That was a misstep on his part," Maddy said with diplomacy. "That offer is retracted, by the way. It was made without the proper context, and now it's off the table."

"What a prince," I said.

She sighed. "Just let me continue, okay? Hank trusted Clayton —so much so, by the end, that he left Clayton everything."

I went still. "Everything?"

"Everything," Maddy said.

I leaned back on the sofa. That pissed me off. Not for me, but for my sisters. Ronnie could probably use money. And Sabrina— she was spoiled, sure, but according to her TV show she was used to a pretty high lifestyle. Bea didn't have a career or a job that I knew of. Disinheriting them was a dick move—a typically Hank move.

"Go on," I told Maddy.

"I think you know," Maddy said, "that Clayton and your sister Ronnie had a thing. They were going to get married, but she took off after the engagement party and stayed away. After Hank died, Clayton tracked down Ronnie, and I suppose they worked it out, because they're getting married in two weeks."

I was silent. The truth was, until I'd seen the story about Sabrina being kidnapped at the engagement party, I hadn't known that Ronnie was actually going to go through with marrying that asshole. I thought the letter had taken care of that—and I was wrong. Because I'd been off the grid, and I'd been busy—doing what? Getting drunk and throwing other drunks out of a backwater bar in Panama. Pretending the world didn't exist instead of facing it.

But now I knew what was happening, and I could put the pieces together for myself. "She's marrying him to keep the inheritance," I said to Maddy.

Maddy kept her expression neutral. Like she claimed, she was a very, very good lawyer. "They're in love. For real this time, and I've spent enough time with them that I believe it. And yes, if Ronnie marries Clayton, the money stays in the family. Ronnie is worried about Sabrina and Bea both, financially. Sabrina doesn't have a job since she left her TV show. And Bea had some problems with a felonious boyfriend and a lot of debt." She stood up to refresh her drink. "The fact is, disinheritance would be a problem for both of them."

"So Ronnie took the fall," I said. That sounded so much like Ronnie, the responsible one. "She gave herself to this guy to keep the money."

"Not much of a sacrifice," Maddy commented. "She's in love with him. Clayton is hardly unattractive, and he's rich as God."

I leaned back on the couch. "Your type of man, is he?"

She gave me one of her icy looks. "I don't have a type."

Sure. I'd told myself the same thing before I laid eyes on her. "In any case, Ronnie is marrying this guy. The money stays in the family. Which leaves me nothing."

"I'm getting to that." Maddy sat down again, and I let my gaze wander her long legs at leisure. She noticed, and she gave me another cold stare, but she didn't move away. "The will was very specific about you," she said. "Hank stated that if you return to the States within six months of his death, you get a significant benefit."

I did the math in my head, and she watched me do it. In two weeks it would be six months to the day. "What benefit?"

"You can stake a legal claim and it will be upheld according to the terms of the will."

She'd lost me. "A legal claim to what?"

She sipped her drink. "To everything."

I stared at her for a long, silent minute. "What the hell does that mean?"

"It means that if you want it, you get everything," she said. "The businesses, the holdings, the stock portfolio, the real estate. The King's Land, the LA penthouse, the New York property investments, the bank accounts—all of it. If you stake a claim, you get everything except for twenty worthless acres. Marriage or no marriage. It's all yours."

My stomach dropped. My chest was tight. "You have got to be fucking kidding me," I said.

Maddy only stared at me from her dark-lashed eyes without a speck of emotion. "I never kid about business, Mr. King."

"I told you, my name is Dylan."

She blinked once. "Then I never kid, Dylan. Ever."

I looked away, out the floor-to-ceiling windows, unseeing. The LA cityscape was nothing to me. I just stared, my brain ticking over. There was one thought that rose above the jumble of the rest. *What did Hank want?*

This wasn't a gesture of my father's love—I knew that much. I knew it to my bones. Some part of him may have thought he cared about me, but Hank King didn't know how to love. A lack that he had passed on to me. I didn't know how to love, either, and it took one to know one.

So he hadn't left me everything out of affection. He hadn't left it to me because it was best for his businesses. I'd never run a business in my life and I had no idea how to start. He'd left all of his holdings to a man who knew how to get into an armed building in the middle of the night without tripping the sensors, a man who knew how to load an automatic rifle in seconds with barely a sound, a man who knew how to sleep in fifteen-minute increments while watching a top-secret location for days. He hadn't left it to a man who knew how to invest and accumulate dividends.

It was a *fuck you* to someone, I was sure of it. His board of directors? His daughters? My mother? This Clayton guy? Maybe all of them at once. It had nothing to do with me.

"I suppose you're wondering why," Maddy said, her calm voice breaking into my thoughts.

She was cool, this woman. Unfeeling, maybe. But in this moment, when I was learning the most surprising news of my life, unfeeling was what I wanted. What I appreciated. I turned away from the window and looked at her. "I suppose I am," I said.

She smoothed her hair back behind her shoulders, a gesture that was unintentionally sexy. I wanted that hair draped over me while she rode me. I very much hadn't forgotten that, even in this crazy moment. "You're his son," she said. "His only male heir. Hank put a lot of importance on that. So much so that I think your sisters felt excluded. They tried to please him, especially Sabrina, but they never could. Hank talked a lot about you, Dylan. About what you would do when you came back. What would happen when his son returned."

I stared at her, incredulous. "You're saying that he left me his entire fortune, above my sisters who have been there all this time, because I have a dick?"

To my surprise, Maddy's cheeks went pink. Like the mention of my dick made her a little bit uncomfortable. Which couldn't be right, because she must have heard much worse than that. Plus, she'd already seen it. "If you want to put it that way, basically, yes. But it wasn't just your gender that factored into the decision. It was you. He always thought it would be best to leave everything to you and no one else."

I stood up from the sofa and paced the room. It was fucking ridiculous—medieval. What year had my father thought it was? I had no idea how to take over for him, run things.

At the same time, Clayton Rorick was an asshole, making Ronnie marry him for money, and at the same time offering me money to stay away. Now I understood his letter—if I took my measly two and a half million, he got the rest of it. He got the richer end of the deal by far. Two and a half million was nothing compared to the King fortune.

What if Ronnie was unhappy? What if she didn't want to marry him? What if Clayton planned to run my father's legacy into the ground or cut it up and sell it off? What if he was an idiot and ended up bankrupting King Industries?

I shouldn't care. I *hadn't* cared for over a decade now. This wasn't my heritage; I'd never planned to take the reins. I'd never thought there was a chance in hell this would happen.

And yet...

And yet it had.

If you stake a claim, you get everything.

I wasn't greedy, though there was no denying that this was a lot of money. It was also a lot of things that were more than money—businesses that employed people, land that had worth. In the wrong hands, if the assets were run into the ground, it could affect a lot of people.

I could live out of one bag for the rest of my life. I preferred it, actually. But I'd been bored in the jungle. I was used to action. I was used to being the guy who parachuted into a bad situation and made everything better. I could do that right now for my sisters, be the superhero who showed up, took care of them, and vanquished the bad guys.

All I had to do was claim an inheritance I had never asked for.

My sisters didn't even know I was in the country. But here I was, thinking about taking King Industries.

I stopped pacing and looked at Maddy. Her honey-brown hair, her high cheekbones, her soft mouth. She wasn't flirting now, wasn't sparring with me. The mask of pure business was on. Her phone buzzed and she glanced at it. Then she put down her glass and stood. Her heels clicked as she crossed the floor toward me.

"Take some time," she said. "Think about what you want to do."

"I don't need time," I said.

She paused, her eyebrows rising. "You don't?"

"Who was that on your phone?" A husband? She didn't wear a wedding ring. A boyfriend? Hell—a girlfriend?

"None of your business," she said. "And that isn't the topic of discussion."

"It seemed important."

"Messages from my fellow partners in the firm usually are."

I wondered if she was telling the truth. Why would she lie? I was very fucking curious. "You want to know what I plan to do about the will?" I asked her.

She pressed her lips into a line, but I wasn't fooled. The spark in her eyes gave her away. I wasn't the only one in this room who was very fucking curious. But she said, "Since it's the main business of my entire firm right now, yes, I'd like to know the decision you arrived at so quickly."

I smiled at her. Decisiveness was a virtue in SpecOps. You were given information and you made a decision about what to do with it. If you waited, people died. "I think the answer is obvious," I said to her.

"And what answer is that?"

"My father wanted it, and I have nothing else to do," I said. "Everything's a mess, and someone has to fix it. That someone is me. It looks like I'm taking over the estate."

6

MADDY

WHAT KIND of man made a decision like that without thinking about it? For all my research, I hadn't really had a full read on Dylan King. Until now, when I finally had him in front of me, in person. Clothed, which was unfortunate—though I'd never admit it.

"You just got off a plane a short while ago," I said. "You should take more time."

"I told you, I don't need any time," Dylan said. "I'm in."

He couldn't be serious. "You would be taking over a massive estate ahead of Clayton and your sisters."

Dylan walked to the sofa and sat on it, his elbows on his knees. "I'll take care of my sisters. Believe me, they won't go without." He turned and looked at me, his dark eyes watching my face. "You don't want me to do this," he said.

I dropped my eyes, turned away. I hated being read like that. "What I think doesn't matter."

"It does, actually. You wanted me to say no."

"I'm just surprised, that's all."

"Why?"

Because I didn't think you were greedy. I didn't think you would take the lion's share away from everyone else. I didn't think you were like that. I thought you were the one person I'd met who didn't care about money. "Like I say, it's a big decision. I thought you would think it through. This doesn't seem like something you'd do."

A muscle ticked in his jaw and his eyes went hard. "You don't know me," he said.

He was right. I wasn't even supposed to know him as well as I did. I kept slipping up, including when I'd handed him a whiskey. I knew that was his favorite drink because one of his exes had written it in an email we intercepted: *Come back and I'll pour you a whiskey, just like you like it best.* It had been second nature to pour him that drink, to try and outdo whoever she was. Thank God he hadn't noticed.

"I know your military record," I said to him. "I know you're a man of action, not a businessman. I thought that taking over King Industries would be uninteresting to you. I suppose I was wrong."

"You're right," Dylan said. "I'm not a businessman. But if I don't take over King Industries, no one does."

"Clayton Rorick will take over if you don't. There will be someone at the helm."

"Clayton Rorick is an asshole," Dylan said.

"He's perfectly competent."

"Competent and heartless."

"Your father trusted him."

"My father made a lot of mistakes," Dylan said. "Screwing my mother was one of them. Maybe trusting Clayton Rorick is another."

I opened my mouth, then shut it again. This was how it was going to be, then. He wasn't going to take my counsel—even though I knew this particular game, and the players, much better than he did. He was going to ignore me and do whatever the hell he wanted.

I hadn't thought I cared.

He stood up, came toward me. Even barefoot—especially barefoot, perhaps—he still seemed like a dangerous jungle cat.

"I get it," he said. "I haven't been around. That's true. Maybe you wonder why I left. Hell, I don't know—maybe everyone wonders."

I did wonder. There was a lot in his file about what he did, but nothing at all about why. "It isn't my business," I said.

"I had reasons. Good ones. My parents may be rich, but they were so toxic they nearly drowned me. My mother raised me on a diet of nasty arguments and insults, and Hank was no better. By the time I was old enough to enlist, I was ready to get away from both of them. I felt like I needed air."

I nodded mechanically, but I could feel my pulse in my neck. That was in the file—there had been a bitter custody battle for Dylan when he was small, and his mother, Charlene, had won. Hank had never had anything good to say about Charlene, and she had phoned my office a few times, livid and insulting. It wouldn't have been a healthy atmosphere for any kid.

And I knew what that felt like. I knew the feeling of toxic parents, of needing air. But I swallowed the words back, kept it professional.

"So I left," Dylan said. "I won't get into it, but I saved a lot of lives. Took a few of them, too. That's what I did, who I was. And now..." He stopped moving forward and went still. "Now Hank is dead, and staying away is a coward's move. If someone needs to take over, and that someone is me, then I'll take over and do the best I can. King Industries employs a lot of people who count on it. My career in the armed forces is done. It's time for me to take over."

I had to remember that this was a job. He was just a client—

not even that, not until the takeover was official. "I'll start the process of drawing up the papers," I said.

Dylan gave me half a smile that made my knees weak. "You do that."

There was a hum of silence between us. If he did this, if this happened, it wouldn't just change his sisters' lives—it would change mine. He'd be my client going forward. My boss. For as long as King Industries employed the firm, which could be forever.

And I'd have to be professional with him, day in and day out. Did I think I could do that?

I had to. So of course I could fucking do it.

I picked up my purse and pulled out a business card. I wrote a number on the back.

"This is my personal cell number." I put the card on the table. "Take the night to think about it and call me. I'll do what you say. And then I'll send you a bill. Because that's what I do, Dylan. That's *all* I do."

He didn't speak. But I felt him watch me as I turned and walked out the door.

～

I WAITED until I was in the elevator to look at my phone again.

I looked at the text that had come in from Malick Gray, the firm's senior partner. *Madison, call me immediately.*

I'd known Malick since I joined the firm, and we'd collaborated on some cases since I became a partner. There were two things that were always true about him: his assistant managed all of his communications, even with me. And he never, ever texted.

I swallowed and hit his number as the hotel's elevator doors opened and I stepped out into the lobby. There was only one account that could possibly get Malick's personal attention, and I had a feeling I knew which one it was.

"Madison," Malick said when he picked up. "What's this I hear about Dylan King returning to LA?"

"He's here," I said. "I'm handling it. I just met with him. I've put him at the Hexagon Hotel."

"You told him about the will?"

"Yes, I did."

"And is he of sound mind?"

Malick was so much a lawyer he put even me to shame. "In my opinion, yes."

"That's too bad. It makes this more difficult. I've just met with the other partners. Get him to renounce his claim to the estate."

I paused by the lobby's glass doors, surprised. "Pardon?"

"We all agree," Malick said, as if it were obvious. "We had an emergency meeting, and we're unanimous. We can't have an inexperienced unknown taking over everything. Clayton Rorick is obviously the best choice to take over the estate."

Even though I happened to agree, my defenses went up. "It isn't our call to make. It's Dylan King's call, by the terms of Hank's will."

"Of course it is. But he has to be persuaded to give up his claim. At all costs, Madison. And you have to do it soon."

"Me? Wait a minute—persuading him is *my* job?"

"Madison." Malick sounded impatient, even though we'd only been talking for minutes. "Did you or did you not just have a face-to-face meeting with Dylan King?"

"I just said I did."

"Then he's met you. You're the one he knows personally. And, frankly, you're his type of person, based on the file we have on him. You're a young, attractive female. If anyone can influence King's decision, it's you."

I closed my eyes and took a breath. Same old, same old—this was the kind of shit I dealt with daily, the assumption that I was a vagina and not a lawyer.

Just get the job done, Maddy. Forget the bullshit they throw at you. Let it roll off like you do all the other times.

Besides, I'd just admitted to Dylan that I'd used the promise of sex to get him to do what I wanted. *You aren't so high and mighty, Madison. You know you aren't. You just pretend like you are and hope everyone believes it.*

"I don't get it," I said to Malick. "I wasn't part of this emergency meeting, and I didn't get to vote on this directive. Yet I'm the one who has to carry it out?"

"You would have voted with us," Malick said with the perfect confidence of a man who has been senior partner for over a decade. "It's the best for the estate and the best for our firm. And you've always done what's best for our firm. Unless you no longer have our best interests at heart? That isn't a good quality for a partner."

I clenched my jaw. I was the most junior partner, the only female, the partner who'd gotten the most resentment when I was promoted. The one people liked to speculate had fucked her way to the top—though they never had the guts to say it to my face. I was the most vulnerable partner, the one with the most to lose. And Malick knew it perfectly well.

"Fine," I said. "I'll talk to Dylan."

"You're already on a first-name basis with him, I see. That's a good sign. And don't just talk to him, Madison. Convince him. I'm not betting the firm's future on a vague six-month deadline. I want papers drawn up with Dylan King renouncing his claim in writing. Signed and witnessed. Or we'll be rethinking the makeup of the partnership of this firm."

"I'll work on it," I said.

But there was no point. I was talking to dead air. He had already hung up.

7

DYLAN

I SLEPT FOR TWELVE HOURS, and then I got up and showered again. It was going to take more than one shower to wash twelve years of traveling off of me. I felt slightly better now that I'd rested, now that I knew Sabrina was safe. But I was still edgy and off-balance.

Madison White's face kept coming back to me, her expression when I'd said I would take over the estate. She hadn't just been surprised; she'd been truly shocked. *This doesn't seem like something you'd do.*

Was this what everyone thought of me? That I wouldn't step up when the time came? Okay, it was a little bit justified. I'd bailed early and I'd been gone a long time. But that didn't mean I didn't have the stones to step up if I had to.

You're a man of action, not a businessman.

I dressed, called for room service, and swiped open my phone. Madison's card was still on the table, with her personal number written on the back. I picked it up and flipped it between my fingers, looking at the numbers and thinking.

She was right, but she was wrong at the same time. I could be decisive, but I needed information. So it was time for me to find some.

There was a knock on the door. It was room service, and I put Madison's card down and poured myself a much-needed cup of coffee. Then I picked up my phone again and dialed a number I knew by heart.

The voice that answered was low and curt. "Eli McLean. Who the hell is this?"

"This is Dylan King," I said. "Who the hell is this?"

"Well, well," said my best friend. "I haven't heard from you in ages. You deleted your email address."

"I hate email."

"I get that. Where are you now, King? Vacationing on the Gaza Strip?"

"I'm in LA, actually," I said. "About thirty minutes from your place. Assuming you're there."

There was a second of stunned silence, but I'll give him credit —it was only a second. "Fuck me sideways," Eli said. "You're in the US of A. I lost a bet."

"I hope it was a lot of money."

"It was. You owe me a hundred bucks."

I sat back on the sofa and drank more coffee. It was good to hear Eli's voice—he'd been Special Ops with me for years, and we'd done a lot of missions together. Then he'd been shot in the hip and nearly died. The pain and the recovery hadn't bothered him nearly as much as the fact that his permanent injury took him off active duty. He didn't have to walk with a cane anymore, but his mobility and his strength were limited and always would be. Faced with the choice of retiring out or taking a desk job, he'd retired and come home to California.

"Do you have time right now?" I asked him.

"Maybe," Eli said. "It depends if there's money in it." Eli ran a private security firm now—one I'd done lucrative side work for a few times. The pay was good, but the clients were assholes.

"Maybe no money right now, but there will be," I said.

"Sure, sure. Tell me another one."

"I need intel, Eli. There's a lot on the line. It's important."

He sighed. "Okay, give me the rundown."

"It's complicated," I said. "Meet me for a drink and I'll explain."

WE MET at a lunch place off Sunset, a spot that Eli picked because they served sandwiches and beer. "It's noon," he said, ordering us a round. "That makes it beer time." I didn't protest; the beer in Panama was atrocious and usually warm, which was why I stuck to tequila. Even the whiskey tasted different down there.

Eli had dirty blond hair that he'd grown out of his military cut, just like I'd grown mine. He was wearing jeans and a faded Captain America T-shirt. He wolfed his sandwich and drank his beer as I talked. When I finished, he sat back in his chair and drained his glass. "Jesus, Dylan. That's a story."

"I know," I said. I took a bite of my own sandwich, though I wasn't really hungry.

He put down his glass and watched me from across the table. "Okay, let's get to the bottom line," he said. "You get everything over your sisters."

"Or this Clayton Rorick guy is set to take over everything. Not to mention marrying Ronnie by coercion."

Eli shrugged. "Easy enough to look the guy up, get a background."

"I agree."

"And if he checks out?" Eli asked. "If Rorick is a stand-up guy? Are you still going to take everything?"

"I'll deal with that if it happens," I said. "I want to be sure about Rorick first. My father's estate is big enough to tempt a choirboy. If Rorick is anything less, I'll take over." I took another sip. "I also have to dig into what happened to Sabrina. I can't discount the idea that if Rorick is dirty, he was involved somehow. Or that there's someone else involved who is close to the family. From the little I read in the news this morning, there's some two-bit local sheriff involved in Dusty Creek. Who the fuck is that guy, and how did he thwart a high-profile kidnapping if he wasn't in on it in the first place? I can't let everything go until I know my sisters are safe."

"There should be sources for that," Eli said. "You'll need a contact in law enforcement." I raised my eyebrows at him, and he shook his head. "I'm not law enforcement, man. They hate me. The cops and the FBI always assume I'm up to no good."

"That's because you probably are. Okay, then, but don't tell me you don't have access to law enforcement databases. Because I know you do."

Eli's face went carefully blank. "I have no idea what you're talking about, officer. No, sir."

"I want access," I said. "I need intel."

"Then call up the local Deputy Dawg in Dusty Creek and ask him nicely for it."

"Eli. I want *your* access."

He scowled. "Why should I give it to you?" he said, proving that he did, in fact, have access. Like I'd thought.

"I don't know, maybe because we spent ten years in hellhole after hellhole together. I think I've saved your life, like, twenty times."

"Once," Eli said, holding up a finger. "*Once*. And I could have gotten out of that one myself."

"Sure, because Taliban insurgents are so easy to take down. Especially when they're coming in through a hole in the roof." He didn't say anything, and I grinned. "Then there was the time in the Johannesburg brothel."

Eli frowned, thinking back. "Nothing happened in the Johannesburg brothel."

"I know. I got you out of there before you could do anything stupid. That's why you don't have an STD right now. You're welcome."

"She liked me," he protested.

"Sure. And her pimp wasn't going to put an ice pick through your temple just to get the hundred bucks in your wallet." He was quiet again, so I said, "Access, Eli. Access."

"Fine," he ground out reluctantly. "Anything else I can do for you, your majesty?"

"Yes. I need a laptop with all of your codes on it. I want to know everything you know. I also need a car. Oh, and remember when we worked that high-profile job for the President's daughter a few years ago? And we got paid all that money?"

"Of course I do. We invested that. We said it would be our retirement savings."

"Well, I want my half cashed out. It seems I'm retired."

He just stared at me. "Jeez, King. You don't ask for much."

"There's a fee in all of this for you, I promise."

"There's a fee when you cut everyone else out of the will, you mean."

I smiled at him. "That's between my lawyer and me."

8

MADDY

IT TOOK me until three o'clock to admit to myself that I was off my game. I'd come to the office at my normal time—seven a.m. sharp —and gone straight to work. It was my usual schedule as the Ice Princess partner, the partner with the most to prove. I worked more hours than anyone else at the firm, and I did better work. I made sure of it.

I had money and success. I was also overworked and had sleepless nights, no friends, and I hadn't had sex in—Jesus, I didn't know. I checked my phone history to find when I'd last texted Axel, the personal trainer who was my sometime booty call whenever I needed a real live man. I liked him because he had a nice body, never stayed the night, and never asked any questions. He liked me because I didn't care that I was only one of the many women in his little black book.

I scrolled back. I'd last texted him a month ago. That meant a month with my own hand and a vibrator, if I bothered at all. Definitely too long.

Dylan King's hard, sexy body drifted into my thoughts. I'd turned around quick, but I'd seen plenty. The fact that he was my client and I was thinking about it at all meant that it had been too long. It would have to get taken care of.

Don't just talk to Dylan King. Convince him.

Damn it, I had no idea what I was going to do. I needed a plan. And I needed to stop thinking about Dylan whenever I thought about sex.

I dove into work, as I usually did, but today I found myself drifting. What exactly was Dylan doing in the penthouse at the Hexagon? Was he sticking with his decision? What would he do next? He hadn't called the number on the card I'd left. I'd hired Max to keep an eye on the hotel, to see if Dylan went anywhere, but I hadn't heard from him, either.

At noon I had my assistant, Amanda, bring me my usual lunch—a seared tuna salad from the bistro a few blocks away. It cost $65, but it was worth every penny. When the door closed behind her, I set the salad in front of my computer and opened the Dylan King file.

There was a paper file on Dylan King, but it didn't have the good stuff in it: namely, the photos and the dirt about his love life. Birth certificates and records from the DMV weren't exactly what turned me on. I ate my salad and scrolled through the digital file again, trying to reconcile the facts I already knew with the man I'd met yesterday. The man I'd argued with, flirted with, and seen naked. The man who annoyed me and saw too much about me. The man who might be my client for life. The man I had to convince, somehow, to give up his claim to millions of dollars, a lifetime of wealth.

I put down my fork and called Max, my investigator.

"Maddy," he said when he picked up. Max was nearly seventy, an experienced investigator who always wore a suit. He'd retired years ago, but he needed money to help his grandkids, and I paid him very well, so he kept me on as his one and only client. This gave him the exclusive right, among my business associates, to call me Maddy.

"Dylan King," I said to him. "Is he still at the hotel?"

"He seems to be," Max said. "He went out for a while, but now he's back."

"He went out?" I snapped. "You're supposed to tell me these things. Where did he go?"

"I have no idea. I tried to tail him, but he took a taxi and I lost him. It isn't so easy to tail a cab in LA traffic."

"He doesn't know anyone here. Or does he?"

"I didn't think so, no. But you never know with this guy. He isn't easy to pin down."

"How long was he gone?"

I heard Max take a sip of something, probably coffee. He was likely sitting in his car in the Hexagon parking lot, watching the doors. "A few hours. He got back about twenty minutes ago. Looks like he got a haircut plus a beard trimming. And when he came back he was driving a car and carrying a few garment bags."

Garment bags? A car? Now I sat up straight in my chair, alarmed. "He hasn't received any money from the estate yet. Where is he getting a wardrobe and a car?"

"Beats me." Max took another sip of coffee. "Maybe military pay is better than I thought. I actually admire him, except I also resent him for making me sit in my car all day when I really need to piss."

"He's up to something," I said. Work was officially forgotten. "I need to know what it is."

"I paid a bellhop to let me know if anyone comes or goes from King's room. So far, he says no. Maybe you impressed him, Maddy. Maybe he just wants to dress up for you."

"Definitely not."

"Well, we know his sister's wedding is coming up. Maybe he's dressing up for that."

"Strange, because he shut down his email and never got an invitation."

"Maybe he changed his mind," Max said. "Maybe—oh, shit, there he is."

I leaned forward in my chair, as if that would let me see Dylan from across LA. "What's he doing?"

"Talking to the front desk," Max said. "It looks like he's checking out."

"*Checking out?*" I nearly shouted it. "He doesn't live here. He has nowhere to go."

"He disagrees, obviously. He's coming out now. And, yeah, he's cleaned up. Nice suit. That thing cost a bundle."

"I can't believe this," I said.

"Now he's getting in his Mercedes. Nice dark gray one, too. He just put his bags in and got in. I gotta go." He hung up, leaving me with a dead phone in my hand.

This was not happening. I'd had Dylan King right here in LA, right where I wanted him. I had him on the spot. He was supposed to think over his decision about the will and call me. I was supposed to convince him to back off in order to save my job. Simple.

And now he'd gotten a haircut, bought a suit, and checked out, driving off in a car he almost certainly didn't own.

I had no control over this situation. None.

I stood up and paced to one side of my office, then the other. My assistant wouldn't hold my calls for much longer. I had a one-thirty meeting with a real estate mogul client and I couldn't miss it. I'd never missed a meeting this important ever in my career.

And there was nothing I could do if I left the office. I didn't know where Dylan was going, and I had Max on the case anyway. He'd find out what Dylan was up to. That was what I paid him for.

I should just relax, go to the meeting. Do what I did best and put my anxiety away in a box. I'd open the box later, think about everything later. Dylan might have scraped up some money, but he needed to deal with his father's will. He *needed* to make that call. That meant he wouldn't go too far without at least getting in contact with me. There was no other way.

I closed my eyes, took a deep breath. Tried to fight for control. I had almost done it when my phone rang—my personal phone. The number I'd given to Dylan last night.

I couldn't tell who was calling. I answered it anyway. "Hello?"

Dylan King's voice was low and almost amused. "I lost your man," he said. "Just like I did this morning."

"Dylan," I said, the name a breath coming out of me. "What the hell are you doing?"

"He's not bad, actually," Dylan said, ignoring me. "If you fire him, let me know. I could probably use him."

"No way," I said. "I'll ask again. What the hell are you doing?"

"Getting out of that stuffy hotel and going home. No offense, since I know you picked the place. But it really isn't me."

"You don't have a home," I pointed out. "Not in LA and not anywhere. So where are you going?"

"You'll find out when I get there, I promise," Dylan said. "Do you trust me, Madison?"

No. Yes. "Apparently I shouldn't."

"Well, you have no choice—you have to trust me now. You should have just let me get on that plane to Dallas. Now you've set this in motion."

"Set what in motion?" I asked, my voice cracking. "Jesus, Dylan, please. Just tell me what you're doing."

"Fixing things," he said, and he hung up in my ear.

9

DYLAN

THE SUIT WORKED like a fucking charm.

I hated suits—I always had. But when I woke up in LA, surrounded by rich assholes, about to become a rich asshole myself, I knew it was time to look the part. One of the things they teach you in Special Ops is camouflage.

I drove Eli's borrowed car to the condo building that housed my father's expensive penthouse. I picked up my bags, including Eli's laptop, and walked into the building, sweeping straight through the front door as if I belonged there. The doorman didn't even blink.

In the lobby, I approached the concierge sitting behind the expensive marble desk. "My name is Dylan King," I said to him. "I'm Hank King's son. I'm letting you know that I'll be staying in my father's penthouse for a while."

The concierge frowned and tapped a few computer keys. "We don't have a notification about this, sir."

"Consider this your notification," I said with a smile. I took my passport from my pocket and handed it to him. I watched him examine it, then hand it back. "I'm in charge of my father's estate. Since I am who I say I am, I'll be going upstairs now."

"Do you have a keycard?" the concierge asked me, still wary.

"Yes, I do."

He shook his head. "No one has been in there since your father passed, sir. He didn't use the place very often. He spent most of his time in Texas on that big ranch."

"I know," I said, pocketing my passport, though I knew no such thing. "But I'll be staying in LA for a while to settle the estate, so the penthouse will be my residence while I'm here."

The concierge nodded, convinced now. "Thank you, Mr. King. Just let us know if you need anything."

Score one for the suit. I walked to the elevator and pushed the button for the penthouse floor. The screen asked me for a keycard and a four-digit code. I pulled a card from my breast pocket, swiped it, and entered four numbers. The screen went green, the elevator doors closed, and I was swept upward to the thirtieth floor, my father's penthouse.

Thank you, Eli, I thought as I pocketed the card. I'd used Eli's laptop to hack the building's security system briefly twenty minutes ago. Once in, I'd set up the card validation and the four-digit code based on the parameters of the system. Computer hacking wasn't my specialty—I'd been more of an action type in SpecOps—but I could do a few things when I needed to. For such an expensive building, the security system on this one had been child's play.

I could have stayed at the Hexagon, ordering room service and racking up my father's estate's account. But instead I was here, for reasons I didn't want to examine too closely. It was partly a *fuck you* to Maddy White, because sitting around obediently like her trained poodle rubbed me the wrong way. But I also had the urge to be somewhere more personal than a hotel. I hadn't entirely lied to the concierge—I *was* in LA to deal with my father's estate. In order to do that, I felt like I needed to be somewhere that belonged to the family, somewhere that was mine.

Or it would be mine, if I took over my father's estate.

I dismissed the thought and waited for the elevator to chime. When it did, I stepped through the open doors straight into a penthouse much larger than even the suite at the Hexagon. It was a corner suite, with two walls of floor-to-ceiling windows overlooking the city. It was decorated with dark gray walls and black furniture, highlighted with post-modern paintings of splotches and smears on the walls. Everything was expensive, everything was masculine and a bit depressing, and it looked like no one lived here at all.

I put my things down and wandered into the unused kitchen, the unused bathroom, the huge master bedroom with its massive black bed. Jesus, it looked like Dracula had slept here. I'd have to change the bedspread, I thought as I eyed it appraisingly, if I wanted to seduce a woman into that bed. Specifically Maddy White. If I was lucky, that was.

I left the bedroom and put the laptop on the table, flipping it open. I'd thought it would be strange to be in my father's penthouse. I'd thought I might be uncomfortable in his personal space, looking at his personal things.

But there weren't any personal things here that I could see. The concierge was likely right, and Hank had spent most of his time at The King's Land mansion in Texas. This had just been a place for him to sleep on the days when he was in LA on business —a multimillion-dollar hotel room, as it were. Which was exactly how I was using it.

The penthouse fit me, like the suit.

What the hell did that say about me?

All those years denying who you are, and it turns out you're your father's son. I set up the laptop and woke it up. I opened Gmail, started a new account, sat down, and quickly sent an email to my three sisters:

I'm back in the States. I'm in LA. I've met with Madison White and she's told me about the will.

Ronnie, you're getting married.

I'll be there.

I suppose I should go buy a gift.

See you in Texas,

Dylan.

~

I HIT Send just as my phone rang. It seemed that I wasn't done with family business, because it was my mother calling.

A phone call from my mother always meant that she was either drunk, in a rage about something, or both. I'd tried not giving her my number at all, but made the mistake of telling her that I was in Panama, and one afternoon she'd drunk-dialed the Panamanian embassy, demanding they put me on the phone. After that, I handled her myself.

"Charlene," I said when I answered the phone, because I never called her Mother.

I heard ice clinking in a glass as my mother took a drink. "You're in LA," she said without preamble, her voice drunk and wounded. "Were you going to fucking tell me?"

Jesus, did everyone know what I did all the time? I'd thought I was under the radar, but obviously I was very wrong. "How do you know I'm here?"

"So you're not denying it. You came back to the States after all this time, and you didn't tell me. It's that wedding, isn't it? That awful little whore is getting married, and you just couldn't stay away."

Of course she'd heard about Ronnie's upcoming wedding; it was a huge society event, not a private affair. Though even if it was a private affair, my mother would have found a mole to tell her about it. "I didn't come back for the wedding," I told her.

"Then it was because that stupid reality show girl got kidnapped, right? That sounds like something you'd do. Or you came back to get money from your father's estate. I know it. Everyone on your father's side is just *so important* to you, and I'm not."

The most enraging thing about my mother wasn't that she was sometimes drunk and often a raging bitch; it was that she was often right. She had a bitterness radar that picked up on every little thing, especially if it was a slight. But the best way to deal with her was never to show weakness. "There's some business with the estate, yes," I said, as if the entire future of Hank's multimillion-dollar empire was a minor issue. "I had to come back and take care of it."

"How much?" my mother asked. "How much did he leave you? He didn't leave me anything."

"Charlene, you're married to a millionaire. You have been for twenty-nine years. You don't need Hank's money and you never have."

"That isn't the point," she said, the ice clinking as she took another drink. "He never gave me one red fucking cent when you were born. He didn't care. Then he tried to take you away, the bastard. And now he's leaving you money? It's a ploy to win you away from me. Don't you see that?"

I scrubbed a hand over my forehead. This shit was the reason I'd left the country in the first place. "Charlene, Hank is dead. He isn't doing anything."

She snorted. "If anyone can manipulate people from beyond the grave, it's Hank. And it's exactly what he's doing. Him and that tart of a lawyer he was fucking."

I went cold at that. Very cold. "Enough," I said to Charlene. "You're drunk."

"Well, of *course* he was fucking her," she said, oblivious to the ice in my voice. "How else do you think she got that job? It wasn't for her legal skills, Dylan. It was for her blow-job skills. I bet he—"

I hung up.

I sat for a second, fuming. That pissed me off—seriously pissed me off. I didn't always like Maddy White, but I was pretty fucking sure she hadn't gotten where she was by getting on her knees for Hank King—or anyone. *You seem to have a way with powerful old men,* I'd said when we first met, and she'd bristled. *Is that an insinuation?* I hadn't paid much attention at the time, but now I realized she'd picked up on it because she heard it *all the fucking time.*

I stood up and paced. I'd had to listen to my mother say a few stupid, drunken words, and it had made me angry. Maddy had to deal with this constantly, from day one of her career. People saw Hank the womanizer and a woman as hot as Maddy, and they thought they knew what the fuck they were talking about. They probably hinted, made jokes, talked behind her back. I'd dealt with it for thirty seconds, it wasn't even about me, and I wanted to throat punch someone. To get anything done in a day, Maddy must have a spine of pure steel.

If she was an ice princess, she likely had a pretty fucking good reason.

It brought out the caveman in me. I wanted to go knocking heads, which was funny, because Maddy obviously did perfectly well without me. She'd built her entire career before I showed up —she hardly needed me to fight her battles.

And I still wanted to fucking do it.

It wasn't just the unfairness of it, the injustice. It was her. She was smart and competent, but I knew lonely when I saw it. I knew lonely because I lived it. Despite the years in Special Ops and all the women I'd fucked, I'd known lonely all my life.

It was getting old, that loneliness. My father had lived as an asshole, died an asshole, and hadn't been able to take any of his precious money with him. I'd spent my life promising myself I'd be different than him. Trying to be better.

All I'd succeeded in doing was disappointing my sisters and hiding from everything that mattered.

And at that moment, as if summoned by my thoughts, the elevator door pinged open and Madison White walked in.

10

MADDY

I was angry. Steaming, actually. I'd had to reschedule the important meeting and leave work—something I'd never done. Amanda, my assistant, had barely been able to contain her shock, her jaw dropping as I left the office. People had stared at me as I walked down the hall.

Damn you, Dylan King.

I'd worked up a good brew of anger on my way here, so as the elevator doors opened I said, "What do you think you're doing?"

I walked into the penthouse and stopped.

The man standing there looked like the man I'd left last night, and yet he didn't. *A suit and a haircut,* Max had said. It hadn't done justice to how Dylan looked right now.

The suit was navy, crisp and cut to perfection. A modern cut, the pants slim, the shirt skimming his torso and his waist, the jacket like a second skin. His tie was soft lavender with dark gray stripes, a color that should have looked feminine and instead looked insanely confident and sexy. He was standing at the windows, looking out, and when he turned to me I saw Dylan's face—but neater, the beard trimmed close to his jaw, his hair cut close to his temples and longer at the top. He was breathtaking.

He gave me a wry grin, as if he wasn't in the least surprised to see me. "Hello, Maddy," he said. "I knew they'd phone you."

"Of course they fucking called me," I said to him, trying to swallow my astonishment and not stare at him up and down. "You knew the concierge would get on the phone the minute you left him. And you did it anyway."

"I told you, I didn't want to stay at the hotel." Dylan shrugged. "It seemed wasteful when this place is sitting empty."

"It isn't yours," I said, taking another step toward him before stopping myself. "You haven't claimed the inheritance yet, which means the penthouse is still the property of your father's estate. Which I'm in charge of. Which you knew. By the way, where the *hell* did you get a card and a security code?"

"I have many different skills," he said, somehow making it sound dirty. "It doesn't matter. I'm here now."

"You don't live here."

"Are you going to kick me out?"

I pressed my lips together. I was mad, but I wasn't about to call security. The fact was that, except for getting a card and a code, Dylan wasn't completely out of line. His father had owned this place, and Dylan needed somewhere to stay. So why had he broken in instead of just asking?

I let my gaze flicker down him and up again. "What about the suit?" I asked, declining to answer his question. "You didn't own that yesterday."

"I'm sure your man told you I went shopping."

"With what money?"

"None of your business."

I closed my eyes briefly. "Dylan, just cooperate with me for one second, instead of being the asshole loner. Just for one fucking second, okay?"

I opened my eyes again, and he regarded me thoughtfully. He scratched his jaw. "The money actually is none of your business," he said, "because I did a confidential side job a while ago that I can't talk about. NDAs and all that. I got paid a lot for it, and I saved the money. That's where the money came from."

There was nothing about that in the bank records we'd obtained access to. Obviously there was more to Dylan than I knew. And I was so surprised that he'd actually answered my question that I asked another one. "What do you need a suit for?"

"The concierge would never have let me in dressed like I was. And I need the suit for Ronnie's wedding. I've decided to go."

I stared at him. "Yesterday you were the brother who had barely bothered to see his sisters in years. Today you're going to Ronnie's wedding?"

"Yes." He stepped forward, came closer to me. I wasn't yet used to this new Dylan—my eyes kept trying to see the man from yesterday, the man from the pictures in the file, sweaty and rugged. This Dylan moved like silk, his big, strong body tamed beneath the expensive fabric. I felt my pulse in my throat as I caught a whiff of his scent, clean and crisp and warm.

I didn't usually get turned on by men in expensive suits. I was around men in expensive suits all the time; they were like furniture to me. When I got laid, I liked men who were a little rough. But it seemed I got turned on by Dylan King no matter what he wore. Especially when he wore nothing—a sight I very much hadn't forgotten.

I was so distracted that I didn't notice how close he was coming until he was almost touching me, the trim beard on his jaw level with my eyes. "What are you doing?" I asked, my voice coming out a little panicked.

"Looking for a wedding date," Dylan said. His voice was low;

because he was so close I could hear it almost on a murmur. "What do you say, Maddy? Don't tell me you weren't invited."

I laughed—pathetically, maybe—and shook my head. "I was invited, yes. Out of politeness. But there's no way I'll go. I have way too much work to do to take off to Dallas for a wedding."

But I didn't meet his eyes. I just kept my gaze on the perfect, sexy line of his jaw, because the real reason I wasn't attending the wedding was because I didn't want to stand there like an obvious spinster, sipping a drink with no one to talk to while everyone around me had fun. I'd done it for the engagement party, and I felt like that was enough. I'd learned a long time ago that social events weren't my thing. People found me intimidating, and— well, not very fun. I didn't drink much, I never danced, and I never flirted unless it was with a man I intended to screw with deadly seriousness to take the edge off. I was terrible at small talk and I mostly talked business. The end result was that people didn't want me at their social events, and I didn't want to go.

"Forget work," Dylan said. He put his fingers on my jaw, my chin, and tilted my face up. "Tell me you'll go as my date."

I couldn't breathe for a second. It was the first time we'd touched since I'd so carelessly put my hand on his arm at LAX. God, that had been like a firecracker going off in my hand. This was softer, sweeter, and even hotter. We were so close. I could smell him. I could hear him breathe. I could see the clean line of his neck where it disappeared into his crisp, perfect shirt.

I kept my voice hard and casual. "This is stupid. Why do you need a date at all? And why me?"

"Because it's the biggest event of the year and it's family. And everyone probably hates me. And I don't want to go alone," Dylan said frankly. "I want company. You're good company."

"I'm not," I scoffed. "I'm—" *A bitch. A cold fish. An ice princess.* All the words people had thrown at me over the years. I'd thought they'd bounced off, but right now I was wrong about that. "I'm not good company," I managed to say.

He kept his hand on my jaw. "I disagree. You're the only one who is as much of an outsider as I am."

Finally, I raised my gaze to his eyes. He was stupidly gorgeous, with those high cheekbones and that perfect mouth framed by his dark beard. His gaze was fixed on me, as if there was nothing else he wanted to look at. I felt my eyes narrow.

"What?" Dylan said.

"I'm trying to figure out what you want," I replied. "Is it a game? A bet? See if you can get the ice princess to melt? What do you win if you do it?"

A muscle in his jaw twitched, but he didn't speak.

"I'm not having sex with you," I continued. "I told you that already. You're a client. You'll be my biggest client if you decide to be. I didn't get where I am by fucking my clients, and no matter what you say, I'm not starting with you."

Now his eyes were hard, too, but he didn't lower his hand and he didn't look away.

"Jesus, you're tough," he said, almost a whisper. "I get that. I admire it."

"Stop it, Dylan." Because that was a bullshit line. It had to be.

"Okay," he said, lowering his hand at last. "If you want it to be about business, then I'll put it this way. I want you there with me to help me navigate this. I'm about to make some people unhappy by disinheriting them. I need you there to back me up."

"So you haven't changed your mind."

"I haven't seen a reason to."

Don't just talk to him. Convince him. I bit my lip, then released it when I realized what I was doing. "And what if the wedding itself changes your mind? What if you think differently of Clayton Rorick when you meet him?"

"I don't see that happening, but if it does, I need you to back me up on that, too. I've never had a lawyer before. Is that what lawyers do?"

"Backing clients up at weddings isn't in the job description, no. Usually we just provide legal help."

His dark eyes didn't leave mine. "I'll need your legal help if I decide to stop the wedding. There might be repercussions to that."

I felt my neck go stiff. "Stop the wedding?"

"Of course," he said. "I don't know Clayton Rorick, and I don't know what he's up to. I do know that he sent me a letter a few months ago, offering me two and a half million dollars to stay in Panama and never come back. I don't trust him with my father's estate or with my half sister. If I have to call off the wedding and kick him to the curb, I'll do it. But he might sue. That's where you come in."

Shit. This was bad. "Listen, Dylan."

"I know," he said. "You're going to try and talk me out of it. But Ronnie is not marrying some dirtbag just because she needs the money for Sabrina and Bea. I'll kick his ass out the door."

How was it possible to be an asshole and a hero at the same time? And how was it possible to be hot while doing it? I'd never met anyone like this man. "You can't do that," I said to him. "You can't stop the wedding. You think you can, and your motives are —dare I say it—almost noble. But you can't stop the wedding."

Dylan smiled at me. "Of course I can."

"No, I mean it isn't actually possible." Damn, I was going to have to tell him. I had no choice. "The thing is, Dylan, Ronnie and Clayton are already married."

11

DYLAN

THE WORDS DIDN'T SINK in at first. "What do you mean, already married?"

She winced. "No one is supposed to know. I only know because of my position as the estate's lawyer. But Ronnie and Clayton eloped and got married already."

I took a step back. "They're already married, and they're having a wedding?"

"I guess they wanted the big public ceremony," Maddy said. "Or Clayton did. Something to do with the fact that their first wedding got called off. Don't ask me why they're doing it when they don't need to. I'm not a big fan of weddings, myself."

I paced away from her, processing this. "I don't get it. Does Ronnie think she's in love with him?"

"I've told you. She doesn't think so. She is." Maddy's voice was low. "She says she always has been."

A love story, maybe. Or maybe a man who was manipulating

my half sister's feelings. How was I supposed to know which one it was? I turned and looked at Maddy. "You knew this, and you didn't tell me?"

Her lips pressed together. "Confidentiality, Dylan. I'm trusted with a lot of information, and I'm not in the habit of spilling it. I only told you because you were about to go charging into a wedding, thinking you can stop the marriage. You can't."

"Is there anything else you're not telling me?"

"Probably," she shot back. "Despite what you think, you're not the be-all and end-all. Just because you've returned doesn't mean I'll roll over and jeopardize my career to tell you whatever you think it's your right to know. I work for the estate, not you. Not yet."

I loosened my tie. Damn it, I was pissed. I hated the idea that Maddy had let me talk about this wedding as if it was an actual marriage. That she'd kept things from me. "I'm claiming the estate. Rorick may have worked his way into marrying my sister, but he doesn't have everything. Not yet. I told you to draw up the paperwork."

"And I will," she snapped. She picked up her purse. "But until that happens, I'll act like the professional I am."

"Where are you going?" I asked her. "We're not finished."

"Actually, we are. Here's the deal, Dylan. I'm not going to the wedding. Not with you and not with anyone. I'll draw up your paperwork, but that's all. Just business. If I need a date, I'll get one on Tinder like everyone else."

I glared at her. My back was up now. "You have a better offer?"

"Any night of the week," she snapped. "In fact, I think tonight I'll get laid. I suggest you do the same. Maybe it'll make you behave more politely."

"I am not getting laid," I ground out.

"Then that's your problem." She pushed the button for the penthouse elevator. "Personally, I find orgasms a very good tension relief. You should try it sometime." The doors opened, she stepped in, and she was gone without another word.

Leaving me standing in my million-dollar penthouse, in my expensive suit, my hands clenched at my sides, and my shoulders braced.

Damn it.

I tugged my tie off. My jacket followed. I tossed them on the back of a chair and started on the buttons of my shirt.

The suit had served its purpose, but it wasn't me.

I think tonight I'll get laid.

Maddy White wasn't going to win this round, even if she fought dirty. She was good—very good.

But she was about to find out that I was better.

CLAYTON RORICK WAS NOT A CRIMINAL.

Hours later, I knew it for a fact. I'd used Eli's laptop and done some digging—Rorick's DMV records, his banking and property records, his criminal record—which was none—and even his medical records. Eli had access to things that made investigating someone a dream come true.

And everything told me that Rorick was who he said he was. He came from dirt-poor roots, but that didn't mean anything. A lot of good people came from poverty. He was taking care of a father who'd had a stroke. He had no record and had started at my father's firm and worked his way up. He had no marriages or divorces in his past, no illegitimate kids, no money scams, not even a missed credit card payment. He was even a good-looking bastard, too, if you liked his type.

I took a shot of whiskey and started a new search. This one was for Garrett Pine, the sheriff who had supposedly saved Sabrina from her kidnapper. He was a straight arrow, too: no botched arrests, no messy personal life, no hints of corruption. A

regular stand-up guy. His parents had retired and he had a ranch
outside of Dusty Creek, which he maintained responsibly while
working as sheriff. He had no need for ransom money, or any
other money for that matter. He was even quarterback in high
school. A fucking model citizen. And he was good-looking, too.

I stood up and paced the penthouse for a minute. I was
wearing jeans and a black T-shirt, both rescued from my Panama
bag. My boots were back on. I felt more like the Dylan King who
had spent all those years in Special Ops, kicking ass when it was
called for. Except instead of doing a night op in a war zone, I was
sitting in front of a laptop, looking up two perfectly normal guys.

I had one more search to do.

You're not going to do it, King. You're not.

But I was. I already knew I was.

I think I'll get laid tonight. You should try it sometime.

It was a bad idea—very bad.

But fuck it.

I went back to the laptop and searched Madison White. She
was a straight arrow—I already knew that. I was looking for
information of a more personal kind.

The information was there to see. She'd never been married;
she had no kids. She had a law degree and a career that had gone
straight to the top. She'd never been arrested—yeah, I checked. I
snooped around until I found two pieces of information. One I'd
expected, and one I hadn't.

The first piece was her address. I mapped it and found she
lived in a condo in a gated community in San Marino—one of
Los Angeles County's more expensive neighborhoods, though
she didn't own one of the multimillion-dollar properties. It was
the kind of place for a woman on the way up, who was biding her
time until she could afford one of those places, because she fully
expected to one day.

Not bad, Maddy. Not bad.

The second piece of information was surprising. It came up

when I searched for an arrest record, because the record I found wasn't for Madison White. It was for her father.

Madison's father, George White, had been arrested in one of LA's dive neighborhoods for being drunk and disorderly. Maddy had bailed him out. That was only four months ago.

When I switched to a records search for George White, I found a laundry list of minor arrests: fighting, public intoxication, drunk driving, then fighting again. There was a charge of public disturbance for a particularly loud screaming match he'd had with his wife, Annie, Madison's mother. He hadn't been accused of abuse, but both of them had been collared for yelling at each other loud enough to wake the neighbors.

Madison's mother had a similar list in her history, though she seemed to have one specialty: shoplifting. She'd been collared in malls, Targets, grocery stores, variety stores—anywhere she could try and slip something into her pocket. One report, from a mall, said that mall security had kicked her out a number of times before finally calling in the law. Annie had pleaded guilty to that one and served a suspended sentence, plus paid a fine. And, according to the records, she had been delinquent on the fine until two weeks ago—when Maddy paid it.

So this was where the hotshot lawyer had come from. I thought of how steely she was, how determined, how she never let anything get in her way. Everyone she knew probably thought she was a bitch, yet not one of those people knew why she was the way she was. Because it was the only way to rise above her roots and make something of herself.

I got that. I'd been born with money, but I'd still had shit parents who liked to fight and didn't care about me. I'd joined the military and left the country to build something that was mine, come hell or high water, with both of my parents in my rearview mirror.

So Maddy and I had a lot in common. Except I wasn't

supposed to know any of this—and she'd likely kill me if she knew I knew.

It was a problem, but it wasn't my main problem. Because when I looked at my phone, I saw that it was seven o'clock.

I think I'll get laid tonight, she'd said. It was a challenge, but fuck me, she'd meant it.

Over my dead body.

At least now I knew where she lived.

12

MADDY

His name was Axel, he was a personal trainer, and we'd been screwing on and off for two months. He was perfect for me: he had a fantastic body, he was allergic to relationships, he liked no-strings sex any night of the week, and he barely talked. I knew full well that I was just one of the many women on his phone, and that was fine with me. As long as he used a condom every time, I didn't give a damn.

After my fight with Dylan, I was decided. I'd text Axel. I'd been thinking about it anyway. Dylan's shitty attitude just cemented the decision. I liked sex with my own hand well enough, but I'd found over the years that the occasional session with a real live dick calmed me down and made me less irritable. So I arranged my life around scheduling said dick sessions when I needed them.

I needed one tonight. So what if I'd be blanking Axel out of my brain while he was fucking me and picturing Dylan instead? Axel wouldn't know, and even if he knew he wouldn't care. I'd just pretend it was Dylan inside me while Axel worked me over, and then I'd be able to think straight again.

I only worked until six, which was knocking off early for me. I fought my way home through traffic to my condo, which was silent and clean, just as I'd left it. I never made a mess in here, and I never let a man stay the night. My condo was my sanctuary.

I toed off my heels, poured myself a glass of wine, and texted Axel. *Meet me at Soho Bar in an hour.*

Working out, he replied. He was always working out. It was why I liked him.

I'll be wearing a thong, I wrote. He had a thing about thongs; they turned him on. Whatever did the deed.

He replied with a thumbs-up emoji, which I took to be agreement. Sure, it isn't ideal to offer sex and get an emoji in reply, but did I mention the working out? You accept limitations with a body like that. I sipped my wine and went into my bedroom to change.

AXEL WAS ON TIME. I had put on a little black dress that was sexy but not too slutty. I had left off the bra—I was small enough on top that I could do that if my dress had a little bit of support—and I was wearing the promised thong. Black. With heels. I left my hair down, put on a little bit of makeup—I didn't want to seem like I was too eager—and lip gloss, which was an aphrodisiac for every man I'd ever met. The entire look said *I'm ready to be fucked, but you'll have to work for it.*

The Soho Bar was only two blocks from my place, which was why I picked it. I didn't want Axel to just come over; when I made arrangements with a fuck buddy, I always met in public first. It gave me an out in case he was rude, belligerent, or I simply changed my mind. There's a delicate art to inviting a man for a simple fucking. In a way it's a crude transaction, but it still requires a little politeness. If the man isn't on the same page as me, I leave.

I sat on a stool at the bar and ordered a glass of wine—only my second, because I wouldn't get too drunk. I sipped it and let the dim, quiet atmosphere of the bar relax me. This was a place for grownups, a place where people came to have expensive drinks and talk softly in low light. It wasn't a family place or a rowdy frat bar. If Axel didn't show, I knew from experience that I could pick up a different man—someone not bad-looking and reasonably rich, well-behaved, and likely married. But married men were a turnoff, and I much preferred men I had vetted beforehand.

Dylan King floated into my mind—Dylan as I'd seen him at the airport, scruffy and wild, and Dylan in his expensive suit. Both versions made me shiver. For a second I fantasized that I'd never met him, and he slid onto the stool next to me, and we struck up a conversation...

The man who slid onto the stool next to me was Axel. He was twenty-eight, six feet tall, muscled from head to toe. He'd showered after his workout and put on dress pants, a button-down shirt, and a wash of cologne. His brown hair was wrapped back in a man bun. The man bun wasn't exactly to my taste, but I knew for a fact that Axel completely slayed with women. I was just one of them.

"Hey, babe," he said with a smile.

I smiled back. I sometimes thought he called me *babe* because he couldn't quite remember my name. "You showed," I said.

"A thong," he said, and waggled his eyebrows. "Yeah, I showed."

He ordered a drink, and I sipped my wine. A niggling doubt

in the back of my mind was making me rethink things. I wasn't sure I wanted this man's hands on me or his cock in me. Usually I was fine with it, and this had been my idea, but now that I looked at him I wasn't so sure.

Axel sipped his drink. "I think I'll tie you up tonight," he said.

My eyebrows went up. "I beg your pardon?"

"It'll be fun," he said, giving me a look that I'm sure he thought was seductive. "Maybe a blindfold, too. Then I fuck you however I want and you can't do anything about it. It's like a control thing."

"I would very much not like that," I said calmly.

"You'll like it when I do it," he said, again with the seductive look.

Now I was starting to get annoyed. "Have you been watching the *Fifty Shades of Grey* movies or something?"

"Are you kidding? I wouldn't watch that shit. It's just something I've been experimenting with. Trust me, you'll like it."

I put my wine glass down. "You know, I don't think I will. And I don't think I'm going to find out."

Axel opened his mouth again, and I knew what was going to come out: he was going to argue with me. Then I was going to send him home. It was like I was psychic and could see the future with perfect clarity, my entire evening spinning out before me. I'd send Axel home with hurt pride, and I'd go home and take this damned thong off. Then I'd never hear from him again and I'd have to start over. It was exhausting just thinking about it, and he hadn't even spoken.

Behind Axel's shoulder, the door swung open and Dylan King walked in.

I froze with pure surprise. Dylan was literally the last person I'd expected to see—there was no way he could know I was here or what I was doing. And yet there was no way it was a coincidence. Especially since he came through the door and made a beeline straight for me.

This wasn't the Dylan from the jungle, and it wasn't the Dylan in a suit. This was a third version, in jeans, boots, and a black T-shirt, showered and clean, his hair and beard neat. He didn't look left or right but walked straight to me and put his arm lightly around my shoulders, his hand deftly and possessively on the back of my neck, beneath my hair. For a stunned second I thought he would kiss me. Instead, he turned and faced Axel.

"She's breaking up with you," he said flatly. "Get out."

Axel was frowning, just as surprised, in his muddled way, as I was. "Hey, man," he said. "What the hell?"

Dylan's voice was low and almost scary. "Go home and don't call her again."

I could have moved. Dylan's touch was light; I could have ducked out of it easily. I could have pushed him off, told him to go fuck himself, told Axel to ignore him. I could have slid off my stool and walked away. I could have done a thousand things—but I did none of them. I just sat there with Dylan's hand on me, his arm brushing my shoulders, as my whole body thrummed and woke up, my skin tingling embarrassingly beneath my dress. I didn't even twitch a muscle.

Axel looked from Dylan to me, then back to Dylan. "I don't know who you are, man, but *she* called *me*. I think it's you that needs to leave."

It was so obvious, seeing the two men side by side. Axel was thick and plodding and stupid next to Dylan; Dylan was lithe and lethal and ten steps ahead. In a flash, I understood why Axel was so boring to me tonight. The thought was depressing and painfully exciting at the same time.

Dylan leaned toward Axel. He was lean and mean in his black tee, a body honed by training instead of by gym weights. "I'm being clear here," he said. "Delete her number. Don't contact her again. And get the fuck out of here before I really get angry."

It wasn't even a battle. Axel rolled his eyes and made a few more threats for good measure, but he got off his stool and left. If he'd had a tail, it would have been between his legs. Dylan took his place on the stool next to me and brushed Axel's drink away down the bar, as if it vaguely disgusted him. He took his hand from my neck but he still kept close to me. "Maddy," he said in that same low tone. "What the fuck do you think you're doing?"

I shouldn't be turned on. Blatant displays of testosterone usually just bored me, but there was no denying my nipples were painfully hard beneath the fabric of my black dress. I just hoped Dylan didn't notice. "I beg your pardon," I said, keeping my voice cool instead of jumping all over him. "I'm having a drink."

"Is this what you meant when you said you were getting laid tonight?"

So that was why he was here. I'd forgotten I'd said that. "Did it bother you?" I asked him. "How did you find me, anyway? Don't tell me you followed me like a creep."

"Fair is fair," he shot back. "Maybe I used the same tactics you used to find out when I got on a flight. And to keep your hired man on me everywhere I go in LA."

I shrugged. I'd actually told Max to take the evening off, because having Dylan followed was giving me a bad feeling in my gut. "That was my job, Dylan. Don't think it's because I'm a member of your fan club."

"I would never think that," he said. "You made that clear. But that?" He gestured toward the door, indicating Axel. "That's your idea of getting laid? He isn't even worthy to kiss your feet."

I pressed my lips together. I didn't want to admit that I'd been about to kick Axel to the curb when Dylan had showed up. I said, "Maybe, maybe not. It's none of your business."

"I'll make you a deal," Dylan said. He leaned in, just close enough to speak low in my ear, but not touching me. "The next time you need service, you call me."

My throat was dry. It was time to end this, time to get up and go home. Time to put a stop to something that was starting to feel out of control. But the words that came out of my mouth surprised even me. "Put your money where your mouth is, Dylan King."

He didn't hesitate. He pulled a few bills from his pocket, tossed them on the bar, and said, "Let's go."

13

MADDY

WHAT THE HELL was I doing? I was following a dangerous man—a man who was almost my client—out of a bar and taking him home. Wait, I was *following* him home. Because he was confidently leading the way.

"How do you know where I live?" I asked him.

"I have my sources of information, just like you do," he said.

My head spun for a second. Defensiveness and pure, unmixed fear. Because it had never crossed my mind that Dylan *would* have sources of information—and there were things I kept private from the world. Very private.

My steps faltered and Dylan paused, turning to look at me. "Are you all right?"

We were on the street in front of my building; the glass doors were right there, the doorman looking at us with carefully masked curiosity. He'd seen me leave, and now I was returning with a strange man. Well, that was too bad. "I'm fine," I said, but I didn't move.

"Maddy." Dylan touched my arm, his hand warm and almost gentle.

"What else did you learn about me?" Because I knew Dylan, and he wasn't the kind of man who did things halfway. If he had researched me, he had dug deep. Deep enough to hurt. I raised my gaze. "What did you find, Dylan? Tell me."

He didn't have to. I saw it in his eyes before he said, "I read about your parents."

No lying, no hedging. Just a straight admission of truth. And for a second I was so angry I could have hauled back and slapped him. "Fuck you," I said, getting the words out through a throat that was closing. "You had no right. Fuck you."

His gaze didn't waver. "Tell me off," he said, "but do it inside." He touched my arm, and it made me even angrier that I didn't flinch away. "Come on."

I didn't speak to him in the lobby, or in the elevator, or when I put the key in my door. I didn't speak to him as I walked into my apartment. I couldn't get any words past my throat. I'd never felt like this—like I was glass and I had just cracked, a huge, violent line zig-zagging through my entire being. Through my life. The last time I'd had a panic attack, I'd been twelve years old and my mother had called the cops on my father during one of their fights. When the red and blue lights came through the window, I hadn't been able to breathe. I had the same feeling now.

I put my hands flat on the kitchen counter and leaned on them as sweat broke out on my forehead. Behind me, I heard Dylan close the door.

He came closer, and he didn't even need to speak. He leaned against my back and put his hands next to mine, braced on the counter. His lips brushed my neck, but I instinctively knew it wasn't sexual; he wasn't trying to fuck me. Instead, he was a blanket, a shield between me and the rest of the world.

"Breathe," he said softly.

I choked a breath. It was stupid, of course, to have a panic attack over a man finding out who your parents were. But I already knew that was how panic attacks worked. They didn't make sense, but no matter how many times you told yourself that, it never made them go away.

"What exactly did you see?" I asked him when I could speak again.

Again, his answer was direct and honest. "Their arrest records. Both of them." His lips brushed my neck again. He was warm, so warm, his chest against my back. "I'm sorry I did it, and yet I'm not. You have nothing to be ashamed of, Maddy."

"You don't know them. My parents are trash."

"So are mine. We have something in common."

I opened my mouth to argue, but in a way I knew he was right. Dylan's parents might have money, but I had fielded calls from his mother, drunkenly accusing me of fucking her ex-husband. And Hank, to tell the truth, hadn't been much better. He'd just had more money and had been better at hiding it.

"Everything I do," I said, "everything I've ever done, is to get away from them. To be someone who isn't them, who doesn't come from them. That's all I've ever wanted."

"I know what that's like," Dylan said softly.

"No, you don't. Because you've never done something you're ashamed of to get what you want. You've always done the good thing, the right thing. I haven't."

He laughed softly. "You think I'm a hero?"

"Of course I do. Everyone does. You went off to serve your country. You're the Special Ops version of Captain America."

"My sisters, and the men I've killed, would disagree."

I was quiet. He waited for me to work through it. He was wrong—no matter what he said, he was a hero. He couldn't help it. Why the hell was he still here? Why didn't he leave in disgust?

Well, if he hadn't already, he would soon. "I fucked my law professor," I said.

The words were out there, dirty and ugly. Dylan didn't move. "He said he'd give me a good grade," I said. "He was in his late forties, and I was twenty. I wanted to get through law school so bad. I wanted it more than anything. So I did it."

Dylan lifted one of his hands and stroked my upper arm, as softly as if he were soothing a cat. "Maddy," he said.

"Don't you get it? I fucked my professor. I did everything he told me to. I sucked his dick, Dylan, to get a good grade. My entire career is a lie. Everything I've done, everything I do every day— it's all a lie."

He stroked my arm again. "One class doesn't get you through law school. It doesn't let you pass the bar, either."

He was right. I'd done most of it on my own, by my own smarts and determination. But it didn't change how ashamed I was. "I'm a fake," I said. "I'm always talking about my standards, how I don't screw clients. It's all a lie because of what I did."

"That's bullshit," Dylan returned. "What's his name?"

I pushed him gently off me and turned around so we were face-to-face. He was still so close, with my back to the counter, but I didn't move away. "Why do you want to know that?"

"Because someone is going to get a late-night visit from some very unpleasant people." His voice was casual, but his eyes were hard. "As soon as I know his name, that is."

I shook my head. "You can't fix it, Dylan. It was a long time ago. I did what I did."

"And *he* did what *he* did," Dylan said. "You were trying to get away from a bad childhood. You were desperate. He wasn't. And if you think you're the only student he's pulled that shit on over the years, think again."

That made the back of my neck go cold. It had occurred to me from time to time that my professor probably had a pattern. He taught twenty—something-year-old girls every day, and I was hardly special. But I always pushed the thought from my mind. "It doesn't matter what his name is. You're not listening. I just told you something I've never told anyone, and you're not listening."

He leaned closer and cupped my jaw with his hands. God, how did he touch me just the right way? I was on edge—if he did or said the wrong thing, I would snap. But he stroked my jaw and the side of my neck, and I not only calmed beneath his touch, I felt shivers of arousal.

"I'm listening very closely," he said. "So that's why you waste yourself on men who aren't worthy of you. You don't think you're worth anything more."

I laughed bitterly. "Don't get any ideas. Axel may not be one of my smarter decisions, but that doesn't mean I'm a romantic. I'm not looking for hearts and flowers and promises. That part isn't a lie. I just like to come, that's all, and sometimes I don't feel like doing it alone."

"Understandable," Dylan said. His hand moved from my neck and he leaned in and replaced it with his mouth, his lips dragging slowly against my skin, his soft beard brushing me. My head fell back and I bit off a moan as I felt a slow, warm rush of wetness between my legs.

God, how long had it been since I felt like this? Since I was purely turned on by a man's touch instead of controlling it, telling him what to do and how to do it? His teeth scraped against the soft skin of my neck and I couldn't contain the moan this time. It came out on a rush of breath.

Dylan kissed the edge of my jaw, then the tender skin beneath my ear. "I made you an offer," he said. "I meant it. If you want to come, you call me. Not him. Not anyone. Only me."

"You are so full of yourself," I breathed as his hand dropped to the hem of my skirt and pulled it up.

"I know," Dylan said. "I told you, we have a lot in common." His fingers trailed up the outside of my thigh to my hip and hooked into my panties. "Did you wear these for him?"

I was hypnotized now, my legs going boneless, wanting to open for him. "Maybe. Yes."

"Throw them out," he said, pulling the thong panties down and dropping them to the floor so I could step out of them. "Delete his number. Whoever else you have in your phone, delete them, too. You're finished with him as of now. You're finished with all of them."

His hand was back on my inner thigh, and he was close, so close. "Are you this annoying with all of your women?" I asked on a breath.

"There aren't any other women," he said. He stroked the front of my pussy, not parting it, just claiming it with a possessive touch. "Only you. And this." His fingers slid into me, slicked into my wetness, moving, rubbing.

I moaned again, louder this time. It had been so *long*. And it was always business, me on a schedule to get off as briskly as I could.

Dylan seemed to be in no hurry, but he was going to get me off faster than any man had before.

"You haven't...proven anything," I panted as his fingers moved gently, irresistibly. My hips moved, trying to take him deeper. "You don't have the job yet, King."

"I'll get it," Dylan said, his voice harsh with restraint and desire. A voice that made me shiver and move my hips again. "No hearts and flowers, Maddy. I won't even kiss you. Except here." His thumb swept over my clit and I arched into his hand, sucking in a breath.

"Do it," I said. It sounded like a command, but we both knew I was begging. "Stop talking about it and just do it."

He leaned in and nipped my earlobe, the sting making me jump. "Open your legs," he said.

My thighs parted and Dylan got on his knees in front of me. I was still wearing my high heels, and he lifted one of my legs and put it on his shoulder. At the same time he put his mouth on my pussy and sucked.

I arched, gripping the counter behind me and making a mewling sound. I pushed myself against his mouth, wanting him deeper, harder. But Dylan had control. He pressed a hand against my inner thigh and worked me slowly, his tongue tasting me from top to bottom and up again, exploring every nerve ending. He'd only done it for a few seconds but it felt like a year, I was so desperate to come. "More," I told him.

Still, he didn't cede control. He licked at his own pace, as if he wanted to memorize every inch of me. He reached my clit again and swirled his tongue over it gently, again and then again, and then he sucked on it.

"God, *oh, God.*" I was pushing now, pressing against his mouth, my hands on the counter behind me, my dress rucked up to my waist, my leg on his shoulder, my heels on. It was dirty and decadent and *exactly* what I wanted. It was against every rule I'd ever made—it set the rules on fire, turned them to ashes, and made me glad of it. It was pure pleasure—his mouth, his hands, his big body on his knees in front of me, his warm shoulder beneath my leg. He held me steady and had no mercy, his tongue swirling and his mouth sucking, over and over, just rough enough that it pushed me to the edge and made me teeter there.

I begged him. I begged God. I shouted Dylan's name as my thighs shook. And when I came it was with white sparks behind my eyes, my throat raw from shouting, my legs sore, my hips pulsing. It was soul wrecking and it was absolutely fucking *incomparable.*

For the first time in my carefully made life, I was out of control. And I had the feeling I'd never completely be in control again.

14

DYLAN

At seven o'clock in the morning, my cell phone rang. I was in bed in Hank's penthouse, mostly naked and dreaming very pleasantly of Maddy's pussy against my mouth. I was hard as a rock, but when the phone jerked me out of sleep, the dream dissipated into reality.

I was by myself. That was fine. I had last seen Maddy five days ago, when we'd had that hot scene in her kitchen. She hadn't called me since. That was the deal—I got her off, and then I went home alone.

I rolled out of bed, following the sound of my phone, and stumbled around until I found it. I didn't recognize the number, but since almost no one had this number, I answered anyway. "Hello?"

"Oh, my God." My half sister Sabrina's voice came over the line. "Tell me you're actually coming to the wedding."

I blinked stupidly and ran a hand through my hair. "Sabrina? How did you get this number?"

"Madison White gave it to me. She said I should call you right away."

Of course she had. "Sabrina, it's seven o'clock in the morning here."

"Oh, shit. I forgot about the time difference. Madison said it wouldn't be a problem."

Now Sabrina sounded unsure, and I remembered how sensitive she could be. "It's fine, Brin," I said. "I was up anyway. It's good to hear your voice. And, yes, I'm coming to the wedding."

"Oh." Brin sounded excited and a little terrified at the same time. "Ronnie is going to be so mad. I mean, also happy. But so mad."

"Why?"

"It's her big wedding. She doesn't want anyone to ruin it for her and Clayton. And I already almost ruined it by getting kidnapped at the engagement party."

"I heard about that on the news." I padded toward the kitchen in search of the coffee maker. "Are you all right?"

"It turned out okay. I didn't get hurt. But I don't recommend getting stalked." She laughed, and I could hear in the tone of it that she wasn't over the scare. Not even close. I didn't blame her.

"Listen," I said, "when I heard about it on the news, I came back as fast as I could. I would have helped, but you were already safe by the time I got here. I wanted you to know that."

"You came back for me?"

"Sure I did. Jesus, Brin, I thought you were going to get killed. I got on the first plane that was taking off. It didn't do much good, I guess. But I tried."

She was quiet for a long minute. "Okay," she said, her voice choked up a little. "Garrett got me out of there. I owe him my life. But it's good to know that I had backup."

"You have backup," I said. God, I had so much work to do

with my sisters. So many years to make up for—years that were Charlene and Hank's fault as well as mine. But it didn't change the fact that there was a huge chasm where there shouldn't be. I was just so goddamned bad at family—I didn't know if I'd ever be any good at it, to be honest. Maybe I'd let my sisters down over and over forever.

I didn't really know, did I?

"I also called to warn you," Sabrina said. "The wedding is going to be a big deal. Like, *huge*. There are a lot of big muckety-mucks coming, like CEOs and the governor and a bunch of others."

"And you, the TV star," I teased.

"I'm not anymore, you know. I quit the show. But that isn't what I'm talking about. I'm trying to warn you that there will be a lot of press. Paparazzi. You don't have any experience with that, Dylan, but I do. I just don't want you to lose your cool, that's all."

I was out of coffee. Fuck it, I'd have to go get some. "You mean you don't want me punching photographers left and right?" I asked her.

"I'm not gonna lie, it's tempting," Brin said. "They're a load of assholes. And I know you're this Special Ops tough guy, and you might lose your temper. Just avoid them and don't engage, okay? That's what I do."

"Got it," I said. "Any other tips?"

"Yeah, stay out of Clayton's way. He doesn't really like you, though I don't know why. He doesn't even know you."

Fuck you, Clayton Rorick, I thought.

Still, that wasn't Sabrina's problem. "Got it," I said again.

"Oh, and come stay at The King's Land. There's tons of room here."

That thought made me shudder. I had no desire to see my father's ranch after all these years. "I'll get a hotel. Really."

"Ugh, fine. There's one by a golf course outside Dusty Creek that Madison always stays at when she comes here. Where are you staying in LA, by the way? You don't have a place."

"I'm at Hank's penthouse. Have you ever seen this place?"

Sabrina had spent a lot of years in LA, and she had been closer to Hank than any of us. "I don't think so," she said. "He didn't invite me there. Is it nice?"

I laughed. "It's all black and gray. There's a huge king bed with a black bedspread on it. The pillows are black, everything."

"Oh, my God," she said. "I don't really want to know."

"Me, neither, but it's somewhere to stay. I'll see you in a few days."

"Okay. And Dylan, I guess I should tell you...me and Garrett Pine. The sheriff, you know, who saved me. We're a thing. Like, a serious thing. We've always been a thing, except now it's for real. He's coming as my date."

I sighed. At least I'd already checked into Pine's background. I'd assess him closer when I got to Texas. "That's nice, Brin. I'm glad."

"Are you bringing a date?"

"Maybe."

"You're so mysterious," she said. "It's part of your charm, I think. See you later, Dylan."

I hung up, feeling strangely light. That had always been Sabrina's effect on people—she could put just about anyone in a good mood. It was why she'd made it in TV and had her own reality show, because people just liked to watch Brin be Brin.

But it wasn't only that. She was my half sister—my family. For a second I wasn't a complete loner with no one to talk to. I had someone who was blood who I didn't loathe. The idea was a strange one.

As I stood pondering that, the phone rang in my hand. I answered again.

"This is Madison White's assistant, Amanda," said the woman

on the other end of the line. "Miss White has asked me to call you in for a meeting."

I felt my eyebrows go up. "A meeting? When?"

"In one hour."

My voice was flat with disbelief. "Mad—Miss White wants a meeting at eight thirty in the morning."

"Yes. She has a very busy schedule today, and that's the only time she can fit you in. Are you available?"

Meaningless, my ass. I smiled to myself. She was screwing with me, and I liked it. She'd made it clear the other night that we were nothing to each other, yet here we were. It was a game, and I was ready.

"I'm available," I told the assistant. "I'll be there."

I wore the suit. I showered and cleaned up and did the whole thing. I even wore the tie. I was an expert at fast mobilization, so I was at Maddy's office right on time.

Her assistant was a curvy blonde of about twenty-five whose mouth rounded in an O when I approached her desk, even though she'd been the one to phone me. "Miss White is in her office," she told me when she'd recovered. "She's expecting you, Mr. King."

I walked down a corridor lined with glassed-in offices. People watched me walk by. I paid no attention to them and didn't bother knocking before I walked into Maddy's office.

It was a big corner office, and unlike the others it wasn't glassed in. It was private. She was sitting behind an impressively large desk, wearing a form-fitting work dress that was scooped at the neck and tucked in at the waist. Classy and feminine at once. Her hair was tied at the back of her neck and she was perfectly composed as she watched me walk in. The woman from five nights ago, who wore a little black dress and a thong in a quest for a fucking, was long gone.

I walked to one of the chairs in the office and took a seat.

Maddy waited for me to say something, and when I didn't, she said, "Thank you for coming."

So we were going to play it that way. I was never one for small talk, so I just stayed silent.

Her gaze swept down me and up again. "Should I be flattered that I'm considered worthy of the suit?"

"It seemed appropriate," I said.

"It is."

"I wear what the situation calls for, much like you do."

It took her a second, but she caught my meaning and her cheekbones reddened. She pushed back her chair and rose. "I don't want to talk about that night," she said. "Not here."

I nodded. I could accept that. Maddy had her armor back on, her mask in place. I knew now why she wore it—it was necessary. I even admired it. "So, what am I here for?" I asked her.

"This is a business meeting," she said. She paced around to the front of her desk, and fuck if I didn't look at those long legs, the perfect curves of her hips in her skirt. At least I knew she wasn't wearing that damn black thong under there. I'd told her to throw it out, and I was willing to lay bets that she had.

I knew why she was doing it, but it still burned a little that she was treating me so coolly after the other night. She'd been all white-hot fire when I'd been on my knees between her legs. I could still taste her on my tongue. *Oh, God, Dylan, please, please, please...* That was the kind of thing a man remembered on his deathbed. I'd done that to women before, but not like that. Not with her. Not with a woman who came even close to Maddy.

She leaned on the front of her desk, hesitating, and I said, "Out with it, Maddy." My voice was rough because it was getting to me, watching her. "Tell me what you want or I'll bend you over your desk."

Her cheekbones flushed—arousal, I knew, and annoyance. So it was possible for me to get to her, then. "I called you here to ask you to reconsider," she said. "I want you to cancel your plan to claim the King estate."

That put a damper on my desire, but only a little. I felt my eyebrows rise. "You want me to reconsider?"

"Yes. I want you to relinquish your claim through the will. Fully and permanently."

"All you have to do is delay me a little longer and my time is up."

"I want a renunciation legally. Signed, in writing."

I blinked at her. "You don't ask for much, do you?"

"It's a business decision," she said.

"A business decision? How so?"

"You don't have any business training," she said. "You don't have corporate or management experience. You don't know the ins and outs of the King holdings. You don't know anything about the investments, the dividends, the capital assets, or the tax structure." She stopped, took a breath, as if this was taking something out of her. "Clayton Rorick understands all of those things. He's worked for King Industries for years and worked his way up. He knows how to lead the company and what it needs."

I watched her for a moment as my blood turned colder and colder. "You don't think I'm capable of doing it," I said. "You think I'll fuck it up."

"It isn't that," she said. "You're smart, Dylan, and you're very good at what you do. It's just that what you do isn't running multimillion-dollar corporations."

"And what exactly do I do?" I asked her.

Her cheekbones went red again. "You're a military hero. Someone who has made great sacrifices for the safety of the rest of us. That's a good and admirable thing. But it doesn't mean you can take over the estate and run it." She took another breath, like she was doing rounds in the ring. "Since you researched me, you've undoubtedly researched Clayton Rorick. And you've found that he has nothing in his background that says he's unqualified."

I nodded. Since her investigator had a line on me, it made sense that he had a line on Rorick, too. Too much was at stake if he didn't. "Rorick is clean," I admitted. "It doesn't mean I like him or that he's not an asshole, but he's clean."

"I know he is," Maddy said. "If he wasn't, we wouldn't be having this conversation."

"However, being clean doesn't mean I hand over my entire inheritance to him. Not at all."

Maddy shifted her weight off the desk and stood. "I don't get it. What the hell do you want, Dylan? It isn't money or prestige. It isn't some lavish lifestyle. It sure as hell isn't a sentimental wish to honor your father's memory. So what are you after?"

That was a fucking good question. Leave it to Maddy to say the words that would feel like a knife slicing down my breastbone. Because I was starting to want things that I'd never thought would matter to me: a sense of place, heritage, some kind of belonging. Things I knew a man like me could never have. I pushed those thoughts away and said, "What I want isn't your business. The question is, what are *you* after?"

For a second she almost looked panicked, but she covered it quickly. "I have no idea what you mean."

"You're pushing me hard to do this. Legally. In writing."

"Because I want what's best for King Industries. The well-being of King Industries is important to the well-being of the firm."

"You mean important to the well-being of the firm's bank account."

She pressed her lips into a line. "You don't care about money, Dylan, but a lot of other people do."

"Is this a negotiation?" I stayed in my chair, though every part of me wanted to stand up and take her on, face-to-face. Where I could look in her eyes, feel her breath. "You want me to walk away permanently from the one thing my father wanted. The one thing he hoped for. The thing that will make me worth millions. You want me to walk away, but what are you proposing I get in return?"

"It's a lot to ask," she said. Her tongue touched her bottom lip, then it disappeared again, as if she'd realized what she was doing. "I wouldn't ask you to do it for nothing. So you're right. I'm offering something in return." She took a breath. "Me."

15

MADDY

DYLAN COULD HAVE LAUGHED at me. He could have walked out. It was a crazy proposition; I knew it. I'd just insulted him, told him to walk away from millions, then made an outrageous offer. But he simply sat like an elegant god in that damned suit, his arm hooked across the back of his chair. His eyebrows went up. "What the hell does that mean?"

"I'll go to the wedding with you," I said. "I'll go as your date. We'll go as a couple if that's what you want. And I'll be...yours."

The word hung in the air between us. *Yours.* It sounded insane, but it was the perfect solution. One I'd come up with in five long, sleepless nights after I'd done the unthinkable and given in to Dylan King on my kitchen counter.

I should never have done that. It was the worst, absolutely the worst, idea. I'd broken the strictest rule of my career, the one I'd sworn I'd never break after shaming myself with my professor. I'd built my career *not* mixing sex with business, keeping my defenses up at all costs. And then Dylan had put his mouth on me and I'd given up every rule.

I should regret it, but after five days of thinking about it, I could admit that I didn't regret it at all. I should be looking at Dylan with the cringing pain of a bad memory, but instead I was standing here wondering if I could get that suit off him, and how quickly. It felt different with Dylan. We weren't professor and vulnerable student. We were two adults, and he made me feel like no other man did. I trusted him.

Dylan was cocky and full of himself, but he was also right: I wouldn't be satisfied with men like Axel when I had Dylan around. I wanted Dylan's hands on me, his mouth, his body. I wanted his cock. I wanted the kind of sex I knew we could have—explosive, passionate, wild. I wanted that, and I wanted it *with him.* With the man I'd been looking at and thinking about for years now. I had him within reach, and I wasn't prepared to let him go, let him find some other woman to fuck and please and drive wild in bed. I wanted that woman to be me.

Dylan had made me an offer, and all I had to do was take him up on it. Hell, he'd given me a sample of exactly the kind of thing I liked: pure, no-strings-attached pleasure.

But I didn't want to just snap my fingers at Dylan and have him come service me the way Axel had. I didn't want him to dress afterward and leave to go down his list, which was what I expected of every other man I was with. No, I wanted *him.* It wouldn't be forever, but if I could get him for a short time, I would do it.

Don't just talk to him, Madison. Convince him.

Malick's directive floated back into my mind. He hadn't let me forget it; he'd pressured me just yesterday, demanding a progress report.

There was more on the line here than Dylan even knew. My career. My future at the firm.

But I had the answer. I could have Dylan, and I could satisfy Malick and the other partners. If only I got Dylan to agree.

I couldn't let him know I wanted him. It had to look like I was giving in in order to be believable.

So I watched Dylan's expression while trying to keep my own cool and unemotional. It wasn't easy, because he was watching me and I knew that Dylan missed nothing.

"You'll be mine," he said, repeating my words back to me with an edge of disbelief.

"Yes," I said, leaning back against my desk. I'd deliberately come out from behind it so he could see all of me, including my legs. I'd seen him look at my legs appreciatively, and I knew he liked them.

He wasn't looking at them now. He was looking at my face, which was worse than having him look at my body. I had years of training in keeping my expression a mask, but it was harder with Dylan, harder right now than it had been with anyone else.

He pushed himself off his chair and stood. I could smell his clean smell, feel his presence, but I pretended I was unaffected. "I need to know the terms of the deal," he said.

"Certainly," I said. "What would you like to know?"

He took a step toward me. "Exactly how long would you be mine?"

"That's negotiable," I replied. "I thought perhaps a week. We could negotiate to two if you want."

"I see." He seemed leashed, thrumming with some emotion I couldn't decipher—anger or lust, or perhaps just irritation. He was playing it close to the vest, as I was. "And this possession," he said, "my possession of you. Is it physical?"

I swallowed in my dry throat. "If you're asking if it includes sex, it does."

"I didn't say sex," Dylan said. He stepped closer, right in front of me, his knees nearly touching mine. The urge to open my legs like I had the other night was strong, and I pressed them together, softly so he wouldn't notice. "Of course we'd have sex," Dylan continued, his voice going low, almost to a murmur. His gaze moved over my face, my hair, my neck. "What I spoke of was physical possession. As in, I have you how I want, when I want."

My heart stuttered in my chest and my neck went hot, my cheeks. His words turned me on, but they angered me, too. "I'm a person, not a blow-up doll," I countered. "I don't relinquish my right to consent."

He tilted his head, considering this. "Yet you're at least implying that you'd consent to me. Is that right?"

Oh, he was playing this game. The game I had started. The game I wasn't sure I could control. I was throbbing between my legs listening to that soft voice negotiating our terms. I remembered his mouth on me, his tongue, how I'd screamed his name. And I could tell he was remembering the same thing.

"Yes," I said, managing to keep my voice mostly even, though the word came out huskier than I wanted. "Yes, I would consent."

He pressed on, still in that low voice. He wasn't touching me, but I felt it like fingertips on my skin. "And for the duration of this, say, seven days, would you consent to anyone else?"

"Not if you agree to the same condition."

His dark eyes went hard. "I already told you, Maddy, to delete the other men from your phone."

"And I didn't agree."

"I see. So you've made it a negotiation."

"That's what this is, yes."

"You want something in return."

"I want you to delete other women from your phone, too," I said. "All of them."

Because I knew Dylan King. He didn't know I did, but I did. He attracted women so easily—too easily. Beautiful, glamorous, hot, sexy women seemed to find him like moths find light. I was reasonably certain he didn't have a woman in LA yet; I was absolutely certain that one would find him within days. This was LA, where literally the most beautiful women in the world lived. One of them would end up in Dylan's bed.

That was *not* going to happen.

"So I give up millions of dollars," Dylan said, "and I delete other women from my phone. And in return, you will *probably* consent to sleep with me for seven days."

I held his gaze. Damn, he had gorgeous eyes. No wonder women fell into his bed. "You want me," I said. "I know you do. This way, we both get what we want."

"You want me, too," Dylan said. "Since I can still taste you, don't try to deny it."

I felt myself flush hot. I wanted to put my hand over his mouth, shut him up. I hadn't built my career, brick by brick, without being careful. And even though we were in a private office with the door closed, I lived in terror of my employees or coworkers overhearing that kind of thing.

But I bit back the reaction and schooled my expression. "I was in the mood," I said. "Since you tossed my date out the door, it was acceptable."

That made him laugh softly, the sound vibrating between my legs. "Maddy, you were screaming my name."

"Like I said, I was in the mood. But without this deal, it will never happen again. That will be the only time."

Liar, liar.

If he put his hands on me right now, in my office in the middle of the day, I wasn't sure I'd resist. He watched my face, and I hoped to God the words weren't showing on my forehead like a neon light. *Liar, liar.*

There was a long beat of silence.

"Give me the paperwork," Dylan said.

There was a rush in my blood—excitement, triumph. Fear. I reached behind me to my desk and picked up an envelope. "We can sign it right now if you want."

Dylan tutted and pulled back, standing straight, putting

distance between us. "You work fast," he said, taking the envelope from me. "You were pretty confident I would agree. I notice you weren't so fast to draw up the paperwork for me to take over, like I asked."

"I drew up both," I said. "I'm very good at what I do." I pointed to the envelope in his hand. "Sign that one."

"I'll read it over," Dylan said. "God knows what it says. I want to make sure I'm not signing over my balls along with the right to millions of dollars."

"I told you, I only bust balls when the situation calls for it."

"Right. The rest of the time, you just turn them blue."

I shrugged.

"I'll let you know," Dylan said. He left my office, closing the door softly behind him.

I exhaled a breath and sat there for a minute, gathering my strength. My dignity.

I'd just gone a round in the ring with a tiger. And I might have won.

Maybe he thought I was a coldhearted bitch. That was fine— it was the image I wanted him to have. For now.

Because the fact was, I knew what it entailed to run King Industries, and Dylan didn't. It was offices and spreadsheets and endless meetings. It was schmoozing and networking, golf games and cocktail parties with rich snobs. It was taxes and budgets and projections and capital gains. For a man of action like Dylan, it would be hell. He'd be bored within days, miserable within weeks. If he took over King Industries, it would be the biggest mistake he'd ever make.

But if I'd told him I was worried about his happiness, he'd never listen to me. It was better this way—a straightforward deal. No confusion and no messy emotions. We'd both get what we wanted—he didn't have to know about the pressure from the other partners. And if he thought less of me, so be it. At least he'd be making the right choice in the end.

As long as he signed the papers.

There was a soft knock at my office door. I knew it was my assistant, Amanda, who had seen Dylan leaving and knew my meeting was over. She was coming in for her usual between-meetings briefing, in which I gave her actions from the last meeting and she gave me the details I needed for the next one. My life was endless meetings, not special operations to take out terrorists. And I could sit here and moon, but the day would soldier on.

I stood and walked around my desk. This was what I did; this was who I was. Dylan or no Dylan.

"Come in," I said.

16

DYLAN

I READ THE PAPERS. Though, I admit it, I knocked back a shot of whiskey first.

I didn't feel like going back to Hank's dark, lonely penthouse, so I sat in Grand Park, watching the crazies and the skaters and the other LA riffraff go by and reading the contract Maddy had given me.

It didn't mention sex. That part, it turns out, she wasn't willing to commit to paper—it would be a verbal agreement between her and me. Maybe, if I was lucky, we'd shake on it.

The rest of it was clear, as contracts go. I renounce all claim to King Industries as outlined in Hank's will. In writing. Forever. No loopholes, no takebacks. The inheritance I never wanted disappearing forever if I signed on the dotted line.

I didn't want to run King Industries. I didn't want an office job. I was already itching to get out of the suit I'd put on to meet with Maddy. I didn't know what I wanted long term yet, but in the short term I wanted Maddy. Naked, in my bed. I wanted that badly—more than I'd ever wanted anything, certainly any other woman. And she'd just offered me what I wanted, in return for doing something I should probably do anyway.

Except I still had my reasons for taking over, and my doubts were far from alleviated. Giving everything my family had built over to Clayton Rorick wasn't something I could do lightly. If at all, Maddy or no Maddy.

I was still puzzling through the pages—I'll be honest, I had to Google a lot of word definitions on my phone—when I got another call. Another number I didn't recognize. Not Sabrina this time. Who else had Maddy given my number to?

"Dylan King," I said when I answered.

"Dylan, it's me."

I went still for a second. "Ronnie."

"Yeah, it's me." I heard her take a deep breath. "Surprise, huh? Sabrina gave me your number. I hope that's okay."

I sat up straighter on the bench. "Of course it's okay. It's fine." I tried to make light of it. "Am I getting a call from Bea next?"

"Yeah, no," Ronnie said with an edge of humor in her voice. "I already asked her. She says if you want to talk to her badly enough, you can call her."

I smiled. Bea had never been short on backbone. "It's good to hear your voice," I told her honestly.

"You could have heard it anytime in the last decade, you know."

I winced.

"Forget I said that," Ronnie said. "I promised myself I wouldn't be bitchy when I called you. So that's the only bitchy thing I'll say."

"It isn't bitchy. It's true," I admitted. "I've been a shitty brother." I looked down at the papers in my lap—the ones that would give me everything over her. "I don't know how not to be a shitty brother right now, to be honest. I don't know what would make any of it right."

Ronnie sighed. "Do you remember the summer we all spent together all those years ago?"

I remembered. The summer I was fourteen, when Hank had somehow won an argument with my mother and had me at The King's Land. The only summer I ever had with Ronnie, Sabrina, and Bea. "Yeah, of course I do."

"You were so cool," Ronnie said. "Really, you were the coolest guy any of us had ever seen. Even Bea. Sabrina was only eight, and she can recall every detail of that summer like it was yesterday. She thought you hung the moon."

Sabrina had been sweet at eight. She was pudgy and funny and full of life. Even with my snotty teenager's attitude, I'd been charmed by Sabrina. It had been a good summer, actually, despite the fact that we were all offspring from Hank's various wives and mistresses, tossed together and expected to get along while Hank ignored us. "I remember," I said.

"That's all we wanted," Ronnie said. "A brother like the one we had that summer. That's how things would have been right. It's all you ever had to do."

I closed my eyes. "I bailed on you. On all of you. I know I did. But I'm back now, Ronnie. I can help you. This thing with the will, with Clayton—"

"That's why I'm calling," Ronnie said. "I know you think you can help, Dylan, but you can't."

"Sure I can," I said. "You don't have to marry Rorick if you don't want to."

She laughed, though there wasn't much humor in it. "Dylan, I'm already married to Clayton. And I've wanted to marry him for the past five years. I've wanted nothing else."

I was quiet. I hadn't known that she'd wanted to marry him for so long. I hadn't known anything. And the only person at fault for that was me.

"Ronnie," I said, "if I get everything, I'll take care of you. All of you. I promise you that."

"That's nice," she said, "but the time I needed to hear that was right after the funeral, when we heard what was in the will. But you deleted your email address instead. So we went ahead and took care of ourselves."

I swallowed. I was going to make up for my mistakes, even the big ones. Especially the big ones. She was going to see. "Ronnie, what are you saying?"

"I'm telling you to do what you want," she said. "Do what's right, Dylan. For you, for all of us. You have all that training, all those instincts. Do what your gut tells you to do."

I looked down at the papers in my lap. Ronnie didn't know about the deal, obviously. No one did. The deal was between me and Maddy.

Ronnie could tell me to follow my gut, but it didn't change the fact that there was more than just me who mattered here. It had never really been about me at all.

"I'll see you at the wedding," I told her.

I had a decision to make.

17

MADDY

DYLAN DIDN'T CONTACT me for the rest of that day. Or that night.

Or the next day, either.

I tried not to think about it. The wedding was now in four days, which he was well aware of. If he wasn't going to sign the papers, he wasn't going to have a date.

And I wasn't going to call him.

I worked late—to make up for the night I'd left early, to keep my mind busy and off of Dylan King. Work was my solace, my groove, and usually my happy place. Except now I wasn't taking as much joy in it because I was distracted. Just another thing I could blame Dylan for.

At nine o'clock I finally powered off my laptop and left the office. My feet ached in their heels and my head throbbed, but I'd only stopped working because I had to, because to keep going would mean making mistakes. I'd worked until midnight plenty of times in my career, but I was going on so little sleep that I couldn't do it tonight. Or maybe at nearly thirty I was just getting old.

I was getting old for a lot of things, I thought grimly as I got in my convertible and drove home. All-nighters. Partying. Marriage and babies. My mother had had me at sixteen, and the shining example of her and my father had ensured I never wanted to get married and have kids. I kept waiting for my so-called biological clock to go off, but year after year passed and it didn't happen. I was pretty sure now that it never would. Whether I was made this way or whether I'd been permanently damaged by my parents, I would never know. I only knew that in this, as in a lot of things, I wasn't like most other women. It didn't make me better than them. It just made me lonely.

At least Dylan wouldn't have to worry that I'd get myself knocked up. That is, if he even agreed to our seven days together.

I'd offered him two weeks, and he'd only taken one. As if two weeks with me would be too long. As if he'd be bored and ready to move on by then. It had stung, but only for a minute. I'd get over it, and I'd get what I wanted: the future of King Industries, the future of my firm, and Dylan. If he didn't sign the contract— no, I'd make him sign it. I'd find a way.

At my condo, I got out of my convertible, taking in the sweet, warm night air. I liked California. I was born here, and I didn't want to live anywhere else. It was beautiful and hot, jammed with traffic and freeways, full of assholes, and regularly featured smog, Santa Ana winds, earthquakes, and wildfires. LA was a bitch, just like me, which was why I understood her. She had bad moods and you had to live with it if you wanted to be in the best place in the world. She was worth it.

In my building, I nodded at the night doorman and got in the quiet elevator. There was no one else around this late; my building was mostly professionals who worked nonstop, like I did. At my floor I got out of the silent elevator and walked down the hall to my door. I swiped my keycard and opened it, stepping inside.

There was an envelope on my kitchen counter.

I hadn't left it there. I stopped, startled. I took out my phone and wondered if I should call security or 911. But what kind of intruder left an envelope?

Then I recognized it. It was the envelope of papers I had given Dylan King yesterday morning.

"Dylan," I said out loud, in case he was here. There was no answer.

Damn him. I should call 911; it would serve him right. Instead, pressing my lips together in annoyance, I walked into the kitchen and picked the envelope up. It was unsealed, and I spilled the papers out onto the counter. For a second I stopped breathing.

He had signed the papers.

I won.

They were even witnessed, everything in line. The witness was someone named Eli MacLean. I made a mental note to find out who that was.

And, quickly on the heels of that, *How the hell did Dylan get into my apartment?*

There was something else in the envelope with the papers. A first-class plane ticket to Dallas for the day of the wedding with my name on it, with a handwritten note.

I read the bold, masculine scrawl: *Where am I?*

Damn it. "Dylan," I said loudly. "I'm fucking exhausted. I don't have time for games."

No answer. I walked into the living room, the bedroom. My place wasn't that big. I felt some trepidation walking into the bedroom—what if Dylan was sprawled out naked on my bed, waiting for me? What would I do? I was half terrified, half anticipating it. But he wasn't there.

He wasn't in the bathroom, either. I thought about looking in the closets—what the hell kind of game was this?—and then I got the answer.

I walked back out to the living room and looked through my blinds. He was there on the balcony, sprawled on one of my outdoor chairs, his back to me as he looked over the city. He had helped himself to a glass of wine from my fridge.

I slid open the glass door and stepped outside. "What the hell do you think you're doing?"

Dylan took a drink of wine. "You say that to me a lot."

"You're *in my apartment,*" I said. "I pay hefty monthly fees here, and they're supposed to cover security. Yet here you are. How the hell did you get in without setting off the alarms?"

The look he gave me said that my question was a stupid one. "Honestly, Maddy. What do you think I've been doing for twelve years?"

"I have no idea, because it's classified."

"True. Let's just say I've planted listening devices in embassies without being detected. Your LA condo security team isn't exactly a challenge."

I gritted my teeth and stood there like an idiot. I couldn't decide if I was angry or disgusted or intensely turned on. I had a feeling I knew what the answer was. Also, there was a second chair next to the one he was sitting on, and my feet were killing me. I wanted to sit down, but I was too proud and pissed off. So I said, "If you're finished giving me that little display of testosterone, can we discuss the papers you left on my counter?"

"Sit down," Dylan said, as if reading my mind. "Your balcony is actually quite nice."

"I don't want to sit down."

"Yes, you do. You said you were fucking exhausted. I heard it from here." He tapped the chair. "So sit down."

I felt brittle as glass, and suddenly I was aware of the cracks running through me, up my chest and down my spine, along my neck and my shoulders. I felt like I was breaking apart. I couldn't do this anymore—not tonight. I moved to the chair and sat, biting back a groan. Dylan reached next to his chair and handed me my own glass of wine.

He looked as beautiful as ever, his face half lit from the light in my apartment, half in shadow of the night outside. He was wearing jeans, boots, a gray T-shirt. He was clean, his hair brushed back from his forehead and almost tamed, his beard trim against his jaw. I wanted to run my tongue along that jaw, over the line of his mouth, taste every inch of him. I also wanted to punch him, and I still had no idea which side would win out.

Still, I took the glass of wine and downed half of it. It was even chilled. That bastard.

"Give me your feet," he said.

"Fuck you, Dylan."

"In good time, but not tonight. Give me your feet."

And I did it. I slipped my feet out of their heels and lifted them, careful to keep my knees together so he wouldn't see up my skirt. Which was stupid, because he'd already had his face in my pussy. And I was an idiot, because I'd never forget that as long as I lived.

He took my feet in his hands, his gaze lowered as if this was serious business. He set them gently in his lap and put his big palms on my left foot, one pressing into the arch, his other palm pushing down over the toes. I made a little sound in my throat despite myself. I'd been expecting a fight—I always expected a fight—and instead I got a seat on a lovely night with this gorgeous, infuriating man, sipping wine and getting a heavenly foot rub. I was suddenly near tears, and I blinked them fiercely back. I was pathetic.

We were quiet for a long minute as he rubbed my feet and I tried not to sob. I didn't even know why I had two chairs out here

—I'd never invited anyone to sit here before. I only bought two because it was nearly impossible to find a balcony chair set for one, as if the default was that you'd be sitting with at least one other person. Not determinedly alone, like I was.

But Dylan was here. Part of me was so, so fiercely happy that we were sitting like this, just him and me. That I had him all to myself. And another part of me knew that we had made a deal, and when he'd fucked me for seven days he'd leave again.

When he did, I'd throw the second goddamned chair over the balcony.

He was treating this foot rub like serious business, his brows lowered in a slight frown of concentration. "You should wear flats," he said. "Your feet are in knots."

"Heels are sexy."

"You'd look sexy in Crocs and a paper bag."

I downed the other half of my wine in a single gulp. "Is this part of the deal? The compliments?"

"If you like." He wouldn't take the bait, wouldn't fight. And I felt like crying, so I couldn't stop baiting him. I wanted to, but I didn't know how.

"You don't have to be chivalrous," I said. "You signed the papers. I'm yours. You don't have to rub my feet or bring me wine. I said I'd consent, remember?"

"I remember," Dylan said, his voice easy and low. His hand moved to the back of my ankle, then up my calf, kneading. "Heels affect the calf muscles too," he commented. "Yours are a mess."

It felt good. So good. Not just the massage—which was fucking heaven—but the intimacy of it, the fact that he was doing it at all. I was his, true. But he was also mine.

For a little while.

I stared at him, not bothering to hide it. I watched his face, his eyes, his lowered lashes as he looked at my feet. I watched the muscles play in his forearms, his hands. I was raging wet, and he probably knew it, and he didn't do a thing about it.

Then it hit me. The long day and the stress and the wine and all of it. Why he was going so slow, why he hadn't called in days. I suddenly understood. "You don't want to fuck me," I said to him.

He kept kneading for a second, and then he stopped and raised his gaze to mine. It was dark, fathomless. His expression was tight and restrained.

"I do want to fuck you," he said, his voice rough. "And when I do, you're going to come until you can't breathe. And then I'm going to do it again. And again."

I couldn't breathe now. I just stared at him.

"You're going to wrap these long legs around me," Dylan said, "and I'm going to be so deep inside you that I'm the only thing you feel. You're going to forget every stupid doubt and stupid argument that's going around in your head right now, because those are defenses. When I fuck you, you'll have no defense against me. None at all."

"Jesus, Dylan," I breathed.

Gently he put my feet back on the ground. He leaned forward in his chair and hooked his hands behind my knees, pulling me forward in my own chair until I was on the edge. He pulled my knees apart and put his knees between them, then kept his hands where they were, holding me in place.

"You had me sign those papers," he said, his gaze burning into mine. "I don't know what your game is, and I don't care. I walked away from millions of dollars for the chance to be between your legs for seven days, and I intend to take my side of the bargain. Tonight you're angry, and angry sex can be fun, but you won't be angry when we fuck for the first time. You're going to be begging me. You're going to be wild for it. You won't want anything else or anyone else. Just me."

My lips parted. *You don't have to wait,* I wanted to say. *That's how I feel right now.* The words nearly rose to my lips. But I said, "You're a cocky bastard."

"Maybe." He stood up, still between my knees, his body so

close that I was level with his jeans-clad thighs. I could have unzipped him and taken his cock in my mouth, and for a crazy second I thought about it. Then he tugged me upward and said, "Stand up."

I did. "What for?"

"For this," he said, and he cupped my jaw and kissed me.

His mouth was just as soft, just as pleasurable as I'd always imagined. We hadn't done this the other night—he'd licked me until I came, but we hadn't kissed. Now he was the only thing I could feel and taste, and instead of fighting him I leaned in to his tall, hard body and let him open my mouth. I put my hands under his shirt and my palms on the muscles of his bare back as he cupped my jaw and licked into my mouth, as slowly and as skillfully as he'd licked my pussy.

I couldn't remember the last time I'd been kissed. My texts to Axel, and the men before him, had always been about sex, not romance. I'd kissed Axel maybe once, a harsh, clammy affair that I'd never wanted to repeat. It had only lasted a few seconds before he'd pushed my skirt up and gotten to business.

Dylan didn't even feel me up—he kept his hands on my jaw as he explored my mouth. I couldn't muster the same politeness. I slid my hands down over his ass and gripped it.

He didn't comment, just broke the kiss, tilted my head, and dropped his mouth to my neck, dragging it slowly along my sensitive skin. I shivered and kept my hands where they were.

He took his time kissing my neck, then brushed his mouth over mine again. "Saturday morning," he said, his voice rough. "The flight leaves at eight."

"I'll be there," I said.

"Good night, Maddy."

I let him go. I didn't follow him as he left the balcony, left my apartment. I just stood there, my body humming, thinking that for the first time in years I had no idea what was going to happen tomorrow. Or the day after that, or the day after that.

And I liked it.

I went inside to get ready for bed.

18

DYLAN

TEXAS IN JUNE was already blistering hot. The sun was hazy behind a bank of lowering clouds, as dark and ugly as smoke, but it was still so powerful I felt sweat on my back before we'd even left the air-conditioned airport. Next to me, Maddy twisted her hair up and put on a big pair of sunglasses as we walked to the rental car counter—she had obviously come prepared.

I was in my usual jeans and tee, and she had on a sleeveless dress that wrapped and tied at one hip. It made her tall, curvy body look like a fucking dream, and she'd taken my suggestion and put on flat sandals. We looked like a couple, I knew. The flight attendants had treated us as such, and the rental car woman did, too, giving us big smiles and glancing at Maddy's left hand. No one knew we were actually colleagues locked in an agreement over power, money, and sex—that we were wedding dates and God knew what else.

We'd spent the time on the plane with Maddy's laptop open,

her giving me a rundown of King Industries, even though I wasn't going to be taking it over. It was my suggestion. I wasn't going to be CEO, but I was still Hank King's son, and I wanted to know everything I could about my father's estate. It would make it easier to keep my eye on Clayton Rorick. Just because I was ceding him the top position didn't mean I was going to be out of his hair.

Maddy knew everything about my father's holdings and how they ran. The more she talked, the more she confirmed what I already knew: in any situation, Madison White was the smartest person in the room. I'd bet my abandoned fortune on it. She was not only a legal expert but had a head for figures and an understanding of complex financials. She liaised regularly with King Industries' staff of accountants and tax experts, bouncing issues back and forth. I tried to picture how she must scare the living shit out of most of the men she dealt with in an average day. I also tried to picture what it must be like to be a girl this smart, born to a drunk and a shoplifter who couldn't keep from getting arrested and rarely tried.

But I didn't say any of that. I just shut up and tried to absorb what she was telling me, though, of course, she was right—I didn't have the head for this shit. It was a sobering lesson, and it made me wish I could show her some of my most impressive skills, the classified ones, so I could get my male pride back.

"Careful driving," the car rental woman said, handing me the papers. "There's some rough weather coming in, or so I hear."

Maddy held her hand out for the keys, but I kept them. "I'll drive," I said as we crossed the parking lot to the car. "You just schooled me for three hours. Let me get my dick back."

"If you lost your dick over a few spreadsheets, you weren't very attached to it in the first place," Maddy shot back.

"I am very attached to it," I said, "and so will you be, soon."

"Big talker."

I glanced at her. "You realize you just flirted with me again, right? Like, actual flirting? Do you feel feverish?"

She pressed her glossy lips together, though I could swear she was trying not to smile. "I do know how to flirt, Dylan."

"You also know how to grab my ass, I noticed."

She shrugged. "If it wasn't allowed, you should have put it in the agreement."

I did smile at that as we got in the car. I put on my own aviators. "What kind of rough weather do you think she meant?" I asked as I reversed out of the space, my arm over the back of her seat.

Maddy was already checking her phone. "Thunderstorms," she said. "Risk of tornadoes."

"Good," I said. "Maybe the whole wedding will get blown away and we won't have to go."

She laughed at that—actually laughed. She was already a different Maddy than the one in LA, who'd been defensive and angry and so brittle the last time I'd seen her that I thought she'd break if I touched her wrong. I hoped I hadn't touched her wrong.

"If there's no wedding, Dylan, then what will we do with our time?" she asked.

"You leave that to me," I said. "I'll think of something."

As we drove south from Dallas, the wind picked up. We left the interstate and got on the two-lane highway that led to Dusty Creek, among other tiny Texas towns, and civilization fell away. Maddy turned the car radio on for weather updates; otherwise we were quiet.

As we got closer to Dusty Creek the clouds lowered ominously, turning the day dark. The wind got stronger and I could feel it buffeting the car. "Is this normal for Texas?" Maddy asked.

"I think so," I said. "Though I grew up in Florida, where we have hurricanes all the time, so I wouldn't really know."

"I'm an LA girl," she said. "Earthquakes and fires are more my thing."

I glanced at my phone and saw another message left by my mother. She'd left two while I was on the plane and another while I was at the airport. It was Ronnie's wedding day, which meant my mother was drunk and on a rampage. One I had no time or patience to listen to.

I put my phone back down as Maddy hung up with Ronnie. "She says the wedding is still on, weather permitting," she said. "They've moved it indoors and they're taking down the catering tents. But guests are already starting to arrive at the prewedding reception, so it looks like they're going to get married, come hell or high water."

I'd noticed something as I listened to Maddy's end of the conversation. "You didn't tell her you were coming with me," I said.

"It didn't seem like the right time."

I frowned. "Do you think the fallout will be bad? That Clayton and Ronnie will fire you if you come to the wedding as my date?" I hadn't thought of that angle, and I realized now that I should have.

"Clayton and Ronnie aren't petty." *Unlike Hank. Unlike my mother.* She didn't say the words, but the implication was there. "They know that I do a good job and that Hank trusted me. You might not be the most popular King right now, but everyone will calm down when the dust settles and they know what you intend to do."

"Which you also haven't told them."

"It isn't my place."

She was right. I gripped the wheel, navigating toward our

hotel as the first drops of rain pelted the windshield. "I'm going to tell them after the wedding," I said. "I was hoping to get Clayton and my sisters alone. Garrett Pine, too. We'll tell them all at once." That the estate was theirs. That they had nothing to worry about. That Dylan the Bad Guy, the one who could wreck everything for everyone, was backing off.

Maddy took off her sunglasses and looked at me, but I kept my eyes on the road. She seemed to be guessing what I was thinking. "I also didn't know exactly how to word it," she said. "The fact that I'm coming to the wedding with you. I didn't know whether to say we're together."

"We are," I said.

She tucked her sunglasses into her purse. "For a while. A week, to be exact."

I felt my jaw tighten. I pulled into the hotel parking lot and said nothing. She was right. Were we supposed to go to the wedding and tell people *We're fucking for a week as part of a deal?*

The problem was, as time went on I liked the sound of *one week* less and less. I was all about time limits with women—I never wanted one to get attached. That was easy when you were always moving from country to country, base to base, mission to mission. I could always pack my bag and say *Sorry, duty calls. I gotta go.* And it had always worked for me.

But Maddy was different. And more and more, I felt *I* was different. I wasn't in SpecOps anymore. I didn't have the next place to go to, the next bag to pack. I was no longer just passing time on my way back out of the country.

And I thought I could get used to it.

My sisters were here in the States—the sisters I'd neglected for too long. Eli was here. King Industries was here, and so were my father's properties, including The King's Land. Even without the money and the power of being CEO, I could get used to it here. I had ideas of what I could do instead of rotting uselessly in a Panamanian jungle. Maybe, instead of taking over what Hank had built, I could build something for myself.

What if Maddy could be a part of that? What if we scratched the one-week deal and tried for something more?

Jesus, I hadn't even slept with her yet and I was already thinking these things. Things I'd never thought about any other woman. But to be honest, the mindless screwing had been getting old. It didn't have much excitement anymore. Whereas every time I looked at Maddy, or thought about what she tasted like, I felt things I hadn't felt in years, if ever.

Anticipation. Excitement. Hope.

"By the way," Maddy said as I parked the car. "I've decided that since we didn't sleep together last night, the seven days haven't started yet."

I pulled my aviators off and looked at her. She was sitting with her purse in her lap, staring ahead. Her chin up. Beautiful and dignified as ever, though now she didn't look cold to me. Frankly, she never had. Maddy White was a lot of things, but cold—truly, down-to-her-soul cold—wasn't one of them.

No, she was warm. She tried harder than anyone else to hide it, but she wasn't cold at all. And from the way she wouldn't look at me—the way she kept her gaze ahead, like part of her was worried what I would say—I thought I had an outside chance at longer than seven days. I'd just have to fucking earn it.

Which I was looking forward to. I was no stranger to hard work, after all.

"So," I said, "the seven days don't start until we fuck? That's interesting. If we don't fuck, then the clock never starts at all."

She blinked, startled, and her cheeks went red. She opened her mouth to say something, then stopped. She turned and looked at me, and for a second she looked alarmed. *Alarmed.* Like there was a possibility I'd decide we were going to be platonic, that we wouldn't go to bed in this nice hotel after all.

Her gaze caught mine, and I smiled. *Gotcha.* Her eyes narrowed.

"You are such a dick," she said.

That made me smile more. I picked up my phone and checked the time. "Two hours until the wedding, and it's starting to rain," I said. "I don't want to be early, do you?"

19

MADDY

DUSTY CREEK WAS a small town and not much of a tourist destination. But halfway between the town and The King's Land was a golf course where rich people liked to go. On the golf course was a hotel that was probably the best one for miles. I stayed here every time I needed to be at The King's Land and not in Dallas—like the night of the disastrous engagement party.

The rain was starting to come down hard as we checked in. I could see drops as big as silver dollars hitting the lobby windows.

Dylan had booked us the so-called Honeymoon Suite, the best room in the entire place. It didn't hold much of a candle to the suite at the Hexagon, but it was still rather nice, with a large bed, a big walk-in shower, and a small balcony. If the balcony was only three levels up and overlooked the eighteenth hole, it didn't really matter. *Enjoy and congratulations,* the hotel clerk had said to Dylan when he handed him the keycard. Dylan just looked smug and thanked him.

He really was a bastard.

But for the next two hours, he was my bastard. It looked like we were going to start our deal. After all this time, after years of seeing him only in the digital pages of my files, I was going to have Dylan King exactly where I wanted him. I'd had to negotiate the riskiest deal of my career to get him into bed, but it had worked.

I walked away from millions of dollars for the chance to be between your legs for seven days, and I intend to take my side of the bargain.

I dropped my bag next to the bed and hung up the dress I'd brought for the wedding on a hanger in the closet, pushing the doubts away. The doubts that Dylan was only here to amuse himself. That I was a temporary distraction, like all the other women in his life had been—except that he'd gone to their beds freely, without having to sign a contract. And the doubts, of course, that after seven days he'd walk away and forget about me. That he'd be screwing someone else while I was still hurting over this. Because I *would* be hurting when this was over; I could be honest about at least that much.

So I stayed turned away, pretending to adjust my dress on its hanger. Gathering myself. Rain lashed the window; outside, the afternoon had turned as dark as evening. There was a flash of lightning, a smack of thunder, and the lights flickered.

I jumped, startled. A large, warm pair of masculine hands came to my shoulders, holding them firmly and gently. I could feel Dylan behind me. I went still.

He stroked my bare shoulders briefly, then let his hands run lightly up my neck beneath my hair. I shivered. I didn't try to hide it, just let him feel it under his hands. Honest for once.

Dylan's hands worked gently into my hair and he undid the clasp that held it back, then pulled my hairpins out, one by one. My hair fell down my back and he brushed his fingers through it. I could feel the tug on my scalp as he touched me.

Thunder rolled again. "If you want me to stop, tell me," Dylan said, his voice low but clear.

I closed my eyes. All that bullshit about *having you when and how I want to*—it had been just that, bullshit. Dylan was dominant, but he wasn't that kind of man.

I summoned my voice. "Don't stop," I said.

He ran his thumb down the nape of my neck, then turned me to face him. He was gorgeous in the strange light of the storm, his dark hair tousled, his gaze fixed on me. I'd spent the entire flight this morning trying to stay focused on spreadsheets and dividends and not on the memory of how he'd kissed me. How nice it had been. How much I'd liked it. How much I wanted it again.

Me, the girl who never wanted hearts and flowers. I wanted Dylan to kiss me.

But let's get real—I wanted him to fuck me, too.

He moved his hands down my body to my waist, hooking his fingers in the tie of my wrap dress. He moved slowly—not tentative, but reading me. Paying close attention to my reaction to everything he did. For all his audacious talk, he wasn't going to just strip me and throw me down. He was going to be *nice*.

I covered his hands with mine, then brushed them gently away. I untied the wrap dress myself and let it fall open. Then I shrugged it off and let it fall to the floor.

Dylan went very, very still.

I admit it. I had dressed for the occasion. I had put on a bra and panty set from Victoria's Secret, a lacy design of dove gray trimmed with small pink ribbon in the details. It wasn't something I usually wore. I'd bought it especially for the occasion, because in my file I had an email from one of his former lovers saying that she had shopped at Victoria's Secret for him. I thought he must like it. And if she could wear it, then so could I.

His gaze traveled over me, down and up again. He was intensely focused, as if taking in every detail.

"Christ, you have a beautiful body," he said.

I felt a rush at that. I stepped forward and slid my hands under his T-shirt, placing them on his bare stomach and sliding them up. *Oh, my God, it's better than I imagined.* "Your turn," I told him, trying to sound playful but sounding dead serious instead.

A glint of humor crossed his expression, and he reached behind his neck and pulled the shirt off in one move. "You've already seen the goods, Maddy."

"I didn't look long enough," I admitted, touching the hard muscles of his stomach, running my fingers along the fascinating lines of his chest. "I was trying to be professional."

"I wasn't." His hands dropped to his belt, and he undid it as briskly as he had the first time, hooking his thumbs in the waist of his jeans and boxers as he shoved them down. "I'm still not professional," he said.

I took a step back. I couldn't look at everything at once, though God knew I tried. The trail of hair below his belly button, his hips, his sexy legs, his cock—hard and getting harder. It was a thousand percent better than I'd imagined, and my imagination of Dylan King naked was detailed and very, very dirty. "Jesus, you're ridiculous," I breathed.

"It's all yours," he replied, making my heart try and crawl up into my throat. He stepped forward and I took a step back, then another until the backs of my legs hit the edge of the bed. Still he came closer, all that spectacular male skin, those hard muscles, his cock awake now and very, very interested. Toe to toe, I was only a few inches shorter than he was, my mouth within reach of his clavicle and his neck. On impulse I traced my fingers over the tattoo on his left biceps, the ring that went all the way around his arm. Then I leaned up and kissed the side of his neck, inhaling his skin. He had a scar there, very old and healed over, from God knew what. I kissed and sucked the skin.

Dylan moaned softly. He reached his arms around me and took the clasp of my bra in his fingers. "Take this off."

"Don't you like it?" I asked against him. God, his neck was so warm. I could feel his pulse, the strong, steady beat of it, could taste his skin on my lips.

"It's very nice," he said, undoing my bra like an expert, "but it isn't you."

I paused.

He didn't seem to notice. He slid the bra straps off my shoulders and tossed it away. Then he lifted my chin and kissed me, just like I'd wanted, a long, deep kiss that took my mouth against his. Seconds later I was somehow on my back on the bed with him braced over me, his tongue in my mouth as his body pressed against mine. He reared back and tugged my panties down, throwing them away.

He looked down at me, naked now and sprawled on the bed, my hair tossed against the pillow, and a smile crooked the corner of his mouth. "That's better. *This* is the Maddy I know."

"You've never seen me naked before," I said stupidly. Because part of my mind still thought this wasn't happening. After all this time—it couldn't be.

"Maddy," Dylan said, leaning down to me again, "I see you naked every time I look at you." And he kissed me again.

I dug my hands into his hair. I wrapped my legs around his hips. I bit his lip, and he bit mine, and when I opened my eyes I saw only dim darkness. The storm was raging, and the power had gone out.

But I could still faintly see Dylan, even in the shadows. He broke the kiss and trailed his mouth down my body, stopping at my breasts to take a nipple into his mouth. I arched into him, my breath coming hard, my hands still in his hair, which was thick and soft. *Seven days,* I thought crazily. *I have seven days of this.* He moved to my other breast and I arched again, moaning this time. It was already better than anything I'd ever done with anyone, because I didn't have to pretend or fence or even wear lingerie. I just got to *have* him. And he hadn't even been inside me yet.

His hand moved down between my legs, his fingers sliding

into me, and I knew he could feel how slick and wet I was. My hips pushed up, trying to get more of him, and his fingers rubbed me, his thumb moving over my clit.

He moved up and dipped his mouth to my ear, his hand still moving. "You're going to get what you want," he promised me softly.

"Please," I said.

"I'm not going anywhere, sweetheart." He took his thumb from my clit and replaced it with the heel of his hand. He was cupping me gently and firmly, his fingers inside me, possessive and expert and perfect. "I hope you're ready," he said. "This time is just the warmup. We have two hours. I have quite a bit of stamina."

I dragged my teeth over the side of his neck. "So damn full of yourself."

He laughed softly, and skin to skin I could feel every vibration of it, the flex of his stomach, the warmth of his breath. "I'll convince you."

"Actions, not words."

I felt him grin against my neck, and then he pushed off me, getting off the bed and standing. The lights flickered, on and then off again, and I got a glimpse of the spectacular view as he walked to his open suitcase. He had another scar on his back, just below his shoulder, and yet another, deeper one on the back of his thigh. I was reminded that he'd spent twelve years fighting, risking his body and his life. He'd done things, been in situations, more frightening than I could imagine. It must have been incredibly hard, taken an incredible level of skill. I admired him, but I couldn't say the words. They felt too raw, too risky. He didn't know it, but he had so much power to make me feel small.

"Did you delete your other women from your phone?" I asked as he rummaged through his suitcase in the dark.

Dylan came back to the bed and I felt it dip as he straddled my hips. There was the sound of him ripping open a box—

condoms, thank God. "No, because I don't have any other women on my phone. I delete them when we're over. Then I change the number."

I looked up at him, trying to discern his expression in the dimness. "So you're going to delete me after seven days?"

"Sorry, Maddy." He took a condom out and tossed the box on the bedside table. "We're going to have business after seven days, even if you don't want to have sex anymore." He ripped open the condom package. "So I'm not deleting you. Ever."

My heart hammered. What did that mean? Was he teasing, or did he really want more than seven days? Or did he simply mean what he said—that we'd have business dealings to do with the estate? I wished I could see his face—though when he wanted it to be, Dylan's expression could be impossible to read.

I wanted more than seven days. I wanted everything I could get. But if I said that now, he'd probably go running for the hills.

Then I was distracted because he was rolling the condom on, and I wanted to see that, too. I wanted to see his hands as he did it, his cock. He finished and slid down, and I felt his breath on my belly, the rasp of his beard. He kissed me there, then trailed his mouth slowly up me, kissing his way to my breasts.

I could barely breathe. "You didn't ask if I deleted the other men from my phone," I managed to get out.

Dylan reached my breast and licked a nipple. "That's because I deleted them myself."

I blinked in the dark. "You what?"

"When you went to get a coffee before we got on the plane this morning. You didn't even notice."

I dug my hand into his hair, meaning to push him away, but he was kissing my other breast, and I just gripped him instead. "How—how did you get the password to my phone?"

He sighed against my sensitive skin. "Really, Maddy. Amateur work."

"Jesus." I wanted to argue it further, but he'd sucked my

nipple softly into his mouth, and all that came from my mouth was a whimper. His hand moved down between my legs again and his fingers slid inside me, his palm pressing me, and he sucked my other nipple into his mouth, and then I was on fire, my whole body writhing beneath him. I didn't care about my phone anymore, because I didn't want any other man anyway. Just this one, doing what he was doing. "Oh, God, Dylan," I breathed.

"More?" he asked, and he sucked my breast again as his thumb moved back to my clit, circling it. "You like this."

I was arched off the bed, and a line of pleasure stretched and burned from my nipples straight down between my legs, where his hand was torturing my pussy. "Yes," I gasped. "Yes, I like it."

Lightning flashed and thunder rumbled. The lights flickered on and off again. But Dylan didn't stop—he just kept pushing me, higher and higher. "Give me more, Maddy," he said, his voice low. "Give me more."

I couldn't think anymore. I could only feel, only push against him as pleasure sparked through me. The pleasure he gave me was hard, relentless, demanding. He wasn't tentative. He pushed me until it almost hurt, which was where I needed to be. My nipples were raw and my pussy was slicking his fingers, and he still wasn't inside me. "Dylan," I gasped, "I'm going to—I'm going to—"

His mouth left my breast and then his breath was in my ear. "You're going to what, Maddy? Say it."

I never thought of disobeying. "I'm going to come," I said. "I'm going to come."

He kissed my mouth, deep and possessive. "Hard," he said against my lips.

I was at the edge, tipped almost over. He put his hand on the back of my knee, pushing my leg up, and thrust into me, the angle deep and powerful. The orgasm pulsed through me and I cried out, not caring if anyone could hear me, not caring if someone came to the door. My body took over and I felt myself squeeze him, the pleasure bearing down as I bucked my hips. He pinned me to the bed as I came and stroked me in a fierce rhythm, his breath coming harsh.

"Fuck, Maddy," he said, on the edge of control. "My God."

"Don't stop," I said. Begging him. He kept stroking me as my orgasm spun out and out, the muscles in his arms rigid and trembling, his face bent to my neck. When I slowed down he pushed deep into me and came, making a sighing sound in my ear that I wanted him to make a hundred times. A thousand. I wanted to hear him make that sound for the rest of my life, and only for me. Only for me, ever again.

20

DYLAN

The rain had stopped, though the sky was still dark and the wind was howling. The power was still off. I stood in our room wearing my boxer briefs, rifling through my suitcase. Maddy was in the shower, and I kept getting distracted, thinking of her in there. Wet and naked. Even though I'd just seen it myself, because we'd spent fifteen very interesting minutes in the shower—after well over an hour in the bed together. I had to give her a few minutes to clean off after we'd gone multiple rounds. It was the least I could do to deliver on my promise, after all.

I was looking for the folded shirt I'd brought when my phone rang. I didn't recognize the number, but I took a chance and answered it anyway. "Dylan King."

"Dylan."

I stopped what I was doing "Ronnie," I said.

"Yeah, it's me. I was just calling Maddy to make sure she got to

Texas okay and she didn't answer. She must have flown in this morning, the same as you. Have you heard from her?"

I'd heard Maddy's phone ringing from the depths of her purse a few minutes ago. Ronnie didn't know that we had come on the same flight, were staying in the same room. Because I hadn't told her, and Maddy had kept it to herself.

"She's fine," I said to Ronnie. "She's here with me. She's in the shower."

There was a long silence, heavy with meaning. "Oh," Ronnie said at last, obviously surprised. "Is that how it is?"

"Yes." Because after what we'd just done, that was absolutely how it was. Maddy didn't know it, but I was in—and for a hell of a lot longer than seven days. I didn't care about contracts or wedding dates or anything else; I'd delete whoever the hell she wanted off my phone, though there were no women on there in the first place. I was in. She wouldn't give up without a fight, but that was fine with me. I'd take whatever time I had to convince her. And I didn't care if Ronnie, or anyone else, knew it.

"Okay," Ronnie said. "That's... unexpected. I mean, I almost like Maddy, but she seems a little remote. And you're..."

"An asshole?" I said. "You can say it."

"I was going to say mysterious."

"I get that a lot," I said. "Maddy isn't remote when you get to know her." *Not when she's naked and begging me.* "We hit it off. It was going to be casual, but it isn't. At least for me." It was a lot to confess to a half sister I hadn't talked to in years, but hell, it was her wedding day. Maybe she wanted to hear something sappy, even from her asshole half brother. "Is everything okay at the wedding?"

"That's why I'm calling," Ronnie said. "It's probably best if you don't come out to The King's Land right now. The rain has stopped, but the system hasn't moved through yet. They say it's still dangerous."

Part of me was jubilant at the thought of having the rest of the day in this room with Maddy, but the professional in me shut that part up and took over. "Is everyone okay out there? Anyone hurt?"

"No one's hurt. We have about twenty people here, the early arrivers. We shut down the outside tent and outside catering and moved everyone into the main house. The power is spotty, but there's a generator, and Clayton got it going. Now we're just waiting." She sighed. "It isn't going to be much of a wedding in the end. The priest isn't even here—he got caught in the rainfall and turned around because driving was dangerous. So we can't do the ceremony, even in the living room. I'm starting to think that a big wedding isn't really in the cards for me, since this is the second try."

"Yeah, well," I said, "Maddy tells me you two are already married, anyway. Legally."

"We are. But Clayton really wanted to do this. We were supposed to get married years ago, and... Well, it's a long story. You know some of it."

"I know the wedding was off, and then he tried to pay me to stay away."

"Forget about that, okay? Because you've missed a lot, too. We're doing this. It's important to him that I have a wedding."

"I'm sorry it didn't work out," I said. "The wedding, I mean."

"Honestly? I don't care. All I want is Clayton. Even this whole thing with the will and the estate... I don't care as long as I have him."

Shit. I had planned to have a sibling meeting with Maddy after the wedding. "Ronnie—"

"No. Don't. Please, Dylan. I have enough to deal with at the moment. I don't want to talk about the estate right now."

"Okay. Is there anything I can do to help?"

"I don't know. There's some flooding in a few of the outbuildings. We don't have a basement or a storm cellar. We have to deal with the livestock, too. We have lots of food and water for now. There are kids here, and one of them has asthma. A couple of people are older. Some people are risking leaving on their own. I just hope we don't have an emergency or the generator goes. I'll be happier when this is all over."

Fuck. No way was I sitting here while all of that was going down at The King's Land. "I'm coming out there to help."

"Are you sure that's safe?"

"Ronnie, who do you think you're talking to? Special Ops, remember?"

"Right. I forgot you're basically Superman. I can't stop you, can I?"

"No, I really don't think you can."

"Okay then, I'll take the help. I'd like to get some of these people home if I can. And bring water."

"Got it." I hung up as the shower stopped and pulled on jeans and a T-shirt instead of the suit I'd been going to wear. I scrolled through my phone again, making sure I hadn't missed any messages. Half my brain was thinking about where to pick up some fresh water to take out to The King's Land, and maybe some blankets and basic medicine. Where could I get asthma inhalers?

All I saw on my phone were messages from my mother. I'd forgotten about those—she'd called and texted multiple times. Her texts were increasingly drunk: *Call me. Call me! I have something 4 u. Why don't u call me?? Check ur email, I sent it!!*

I sighed and accessed my voice mailbox. It was more of the same: My mother rambling about my going to Ronnie's wedding, about how I was with the "whore lawyer your father was fucking." It was alarming how much she knew about my movements. But aside from that, her disrespect of Maddy made me see red. Charlene was going to learn to keep her mouth shut where Maddy was concerned, or she'd be getting a lesson from me. I wasn't going to put up with that shit.

The last voice mail mentioned an email again. "You want to see what I sent you, trust me," my mother warned. She was a notorious liar—I knew that. She was also a drama queen. Still, as

I heard the hair dryer run in the bathroom, I flipped open my laptop, accessed my phone hotspot to bypass the Wi-Fi, and downloaded the last email that had come in.

It was from my mother. *Read This*, it said. Attached was a file. She was probably trying to give me a fucking virus, but what the hell. I clicked it and looked at the documents inside.

I went cold.

It was me.

The first item was a photo of me on the beach in Panama, walking on the sand. I was wearing swim trunks and no shirt. I remembered that day; it was one of the few days I'd spent on the beach when I first arrived. And I'd had no fucking idea someone was taking my photograph.

The next photo was of me in Panama City, coming out of the bank. I remembered that day, too. I'd withdrawn my pay. The shot was taken from across the street, probably from a car.

The next photo went back to when I was still in Special Ops. I was in a restaurant in Marrakesh with one of my exes, and— Jesus, you could see her foot under the table, where she'd pushed off her sandal and was running her toes under the cuff of my pants. I remembered that moment, too. I flipped through photo after photo, remembering all of them. Then I found more: financial records, military records. Prefaced with a simple memo: *Dear Miss White, here are the documents you requested. Regards.*

She'd had me watched. How long? Months. Years. There were intercepted emails, private ones. Maddy had said nothing to me about this. And yet she'd read all of it. *All* of it.

Part of me understood it. I was the potential heir to my father's multimillion-dollar fortune; keeping me as an unknown entity was out of the question. I'd looked up Clayton Rorick myself, and so had Maddy. It stung that she hadn't told me, that she knew so much about me and didn't trust me enough to tell me how. But part of me, deep down, could maybe see why.

It was the final email that broke everything.

It was an internal memo sent from Maddy's partners in the firm, addressed to her. Everything official, everything in line. *Since we have received the fully executed documents regarding Dylan King and his father's estate, and since you have completed what was requested of you by the firm, we have deposited your bonus.* What followed was a very, very big fucking number: a bonus. For Maddy. For getting me to sign the papers forfeiting my father's estate.

Requested of you by the firm.

I sat for a second and stared at it like an idiot. Maddy had pushed me to sign those papers. She'd been persuasive. And in the end, she had offered me herself. For seven days. If only I signed those papers.

For money.

A lot of fucking money.

Jesus. How could I have been so stupid?

Behind me, the bathroom door opened.

"Sorry I took so long," Maddy said. "I wanted to look nice. Has the rain stopped?"

I couldn't say anything. My throat was frozen. I could only stare at the screen, unable to believe what the hell I was looking at.

There was a postscript at the bottom of the bonus letter. *Thank you, Miss White. Well done.*

"What's going on?" Maddy's voice. The voice I'd heard in my ear in bed for the last two hours. The woman I'd been so sure of minutes ago. "Why are you in jeans? What are you looking at?"

Thank you, Miss White. Well done.

The memo was dated two hours ago.

I found my voice, and it came out low with anger. "You tell me."

She came closer. I didn't look at her, but from the corner of my eye I saw that she was wrapped in a towel, her makeup on and her hair done, ready for the wedding. She put a hand on my shoulder, but she must have felt how tense I was, because she dropped it. "What is that?"

I flipped away from the memo to the photo of me on the beach. "Recognize this?"

Her soft intake of breath answered my question.

"Or this?" I flipped to the bank photo. The Marrakesh photo. The bank photo. "This? This?"

Behind my shoulder, she was silent.

"I guess you do," I said, the words like ice in my throat. "And I know you've checked your email since we landed. So I know you recognize this."

I flipped to the memo, but I didn't bother watching her reaction.

We were done.

21

MADDY

THIS WASN'T HAPPENING. It couldn't be. I wasn't standing here with Dylan—the man I wanted, the man I had just slept with, the man I was falling in love with—looking at that fucking file. Just ten minutes ago in the shower, I'd decided to delete the file because it didn't matter anymore. I didn't need it; no one needed it. And Dylan didn't need to know it existed.

Except now he did. And he was furious.

I could see it in the line of his body, his jaw. The tightness of his voice. And he wouldn't look at me. He just looked at his laptop screen as he flipped through the photos and—

God, it was *all* there. And through the wash of panic and shame in my blood, I also felt a burning anger lit by curiosity. The Dylan King file was confidential. Who the hell had leaked it?

This was the worst, though. I would explain. I had been hired to keep that file; Dylan would understand that. I should have told him about it sooner, but keeping it in the first place hadn't been my idea. This was bad, but it could be saved.

Then he flipped to another document, and everything got worse.

It was the memo from Malick. I'd seen it come in on my phone, seen the email subject—*King agreement*—and I hadn't opened it. I'd assumed it was just an acknowledgment that the partners had seen the contract, that everything was business as usual.

But that wasn't what the memo said. Reading it now, I saw that the partners had given me a bonus. A very, *very* large bonus. For *completing what was requested of you by the firm.*

I felt sick, my stomach like cold, thick lead. "Oh, my God," I rasped.

"Thank you, Miss White," Dylan said, his voice cynical and harsh. "Well done."

No. Oh, no. He was quoting Malick's postscript at the end of the memo. "This isn't what you think," I managed to say.

"No?" Dylan stood and walked to his suitcase. "It seems pretty fucking clear to me. Your partners gave you an assignment to get me to sign those papers from the beginning. And you followed through, because you always follow through. Right? Even if you have to fuck me to do it."

"No," I said. I sounded panicked. I *was* panicked. He was so cold, this man I'd just spent hours in bed with. "It wasn't like that at all."

"You didn't get a bonus?" Dylan threw his clothes into his suit-case. "I guess you didn't keep a file on me for years, either?"

"That was just an assignment, part of the King file. Hank had to know where you were and what you were doing. You were his heir, the heir to everything, and you weren't speaking to him. He had to have updates on you. He needed to know."

"And my emails? I suppose he needed to read those, too."

"Dylan—"

"Copies of my paychecks. My medical records from the military. Pictures of me with girlfriends." He dropped the last item into his suitcase and slammed it shut. "Did you get paid a bonus for those, too? I've been pretty profitable for you, haven't I?"

I felt so naked, standing there in just a towel under his scathing anger. I looked at his profile—because he still wouldn't look at me—and saw a man made of granite. "Dylan, please listen. I realize this is—"

"Maddy, they paid you a fucking bonus."

"I didn't know about it!" I cried. "Malick never told me about a bonus! I swear it!"

"Right." He turned to look at me at last, and his eyes were dark with fury. "He just told you to make me sign the papers that would put Clayton in control of King Industries. He *assigned* you to do it. The other partners, too. And because you have to keep your job, you fucking did it. You followed orders."

I swallowed. "It was the right thing to do and you know it."

"Of course you'd say that. Your bank account is very convincing."

I couldn't believe Malick had given me a bonus. It made me furious, but my anger didn't matter. This had already ruined everything. I had to ask. "How did you get those files? They're confidential."

"My mother," Dylan said. He snapped the laptop closed and zipped his suitcase. "She's a bitch, and she thinks you were fucking Hank. She heard I was coming to the wedding with you and she thinks you have me in her clutches, as she puts it. She sent it all to me along with a bunch of drunken messages about how I should know the truth. If I had to guess, I'd say she got the files from your assistant. My mother has a lot of money, and she always knows who to pay to get what she wants."

Amanda? Jesus. She'd worked for me for over a year, and she'd come with impeccable references. But those files couldn't have come from anyone else, except me personally. The King file wasn't kept on a company server, only on my private one. No one else had access to the passwords. "That's how your mother knows you're here with me," I said. "From Amanda."

"It is." Dylan looked grim. He sat on the edge of the rumpled bed and pulled his boots on. "It's also how she knew I was back from Panama. I couldn't figure out who told her, but now I know." He paused and looked up at me. "Are you ever going to tell me how you knew I was on that flight? Or are you going to keep the rest of your secrets?"

I shook my head. It didn't matter anymore. "Max, my investigator, had a contact there," I said. "A woman."

Recognition crossed his expression, and then he scrubbed a hand over his face. "Funny. I thought she actually liked me. Oh, well—at least she'll put the money to good use." He picked up his boot, then stopped again. "Wait a minute. When we first went to the Hexagon, you poured me a whiskey. I thought you'd made a good guess at my favorite drink. But you didn't, did you?"

I crossed my arms and leaned back against the dresser, silent.

Dylan looked at me, his gaze hard. "You got that from the emails you intercepted. And Jesus—the lingerie. That's why you wore that lingerie. Isn't it?"

I looked away. My eyes stung. I could feel the track of a tear on my cheek, and I took a breath to keep the rest of them back.

"Don't answer that." I heard Dylan stand up. "I get it. You used the information you had to manipulate me, to get me to sign those papers. You had an assignment, and you got paid. None of it was real."

"It was real," I protested, looking at him again. He was fully dressed now, and he picked up his suitcase. "I was just trying to—"

"To what?" His voice was hard. When I didn't answer, he turned for the door.

I suddenly realized what was going on. "Wait. Where are you going?"

"The wedding's off," he said shortly. "Ronnie has a bunch of guests there sheltering from the storm. I'm going to bring supplies and help them."

"I'll come with you."

"No, you won't."

I hugged myself harder, feeling more naked than ever, barefoot and wearing only a towel, unable to follow him out the door. "What do you want me to do?"

"Stay here," he said. "The weather could turn again. There's no need for you to leave."

"You just don't want me with you."

He turned back and looked at me. "It isn't safe," he said, "but no, I don't want you with me."

Damn it. I couldn't even leave, because he was taking our only car, and he knew it. "So you're stranding me."

"Honestly? I don't care what you do. Watch some TV if the power comes on and you can get a signal. Read a book. Use your wads of money to charter a private plane. Whatever you want to do to pass the time."

I flinched. "You really are an asshole."

"Yeah, well, that isn't news. I have to go. I'll send someone back to pick you up and take you to the airport in the morning." He turned away.

"Fuck you," I said, but the door had already closed behind him.

I stood there for a long minute. I felt raw, as if someone had stripped my skin off. Like someone had opened my chest and ripped the inside out. I had warm tear tracks on my cheeks, no doubt smearing the makeup I'd so carefully put on for the wedding.

I twisted a hand in my towel, squeezing it. Fuck it. I didn't know about the bonus. And I'd been doing my job—my damned *job*. The job I'd fought so hard for and clawed my way inch by inch to get and keep. And signing those papers *had* been the right thing to do.

But I knew Dylan now. I knew the object of all my research. I'd talked to him, argued with him, listened to him, been to bed with him. I'd fallen for him. This wasn't a job anymore. He felt like he'd been manipulated, like he hadn't been given a choice. By me. And in exchange for taking away his choice, I'd been paid a lot of money.

Damn Malick. Damn Amanda, who was going to find herself on the receiving end of criminal charges as soon as I could get myself together. Damn Charlene, Dylan's mother. Damn Hank, for assigning me to snoop on his son in the first place.

And damn Dylan. He hadn't even let me explain. He'd just walked out, leaving me naked and in tears. Leaving me stranded and alone in the middle of a storm, so he could go play hero and never have to look at me again. All because I'd let him down.

Slowly, as I stood there, my ripped-open grief turned to anger. Anger at myself for being a heartless bitch. Anger at everyone.

I undid the towel. I used it to wipe my tears, and then I dropped it to the floor and walked naked into the bathroom. I washed the makeup from my face, then brushed out the careful arrangement of my hair and twisted it into a ponytail.

I stepped out to my suitcase and pulled on the only casual clothes I'd brought: a slim pair of dark capri pants and a fitted cream T-shirt. I'd planned to wear them on the plane home tomorrow, but now would have to do. The wedding-guest dress I'd brought would stay on its hanger in the closet.

I pulled on a pair of canvas sneakers and picked up my purse. Dylan might have driven off in the car we shared, but if he thought I was going to sit here and weep into my handkerchief, he was very fucking wrong. I had things I could do, too.

I finished tying my shoes and the breath went out of me in a swoop. I sat with my hands hugging my knees as pain rushed through me, up from deep in my stomach, through my chest. I gasped for air and bit back tears, trying not to sob.

You lost Dylan. You had him, and you lost him.

I didn't entirely succeed in staying quiet. A few sobs escaped me, and a few more tears tracked down my face. It seemed that this was what heartbreak felt like—something I'd never felt. No wonder people lived their entire lives trying not to feel this way. It was horrible and overwhelming, and I had a feeling I was going to be feeling it for a long time.

When the pain subsided a little, I straightened and wiped my tears. Then I picked up my purse and left the room.

I'd had him, and I'd lost him.

But I wasn't dead. There were still things I could do.

22

DYLAN

I HADN'T SEEN The King's Land since the summer I was fourteen, the summer I spent with my sisters. I'd pushed that memory far down, made it part of my past, but looking at the place now brought everything back again.

The house was huge, there was a pool, and the grounds were big enough for a teenager and three young girls to roam. There was a stable with horses—one of Hank's profitable pastimes had been horse breeding—and if you hiked far enough there was a watering hole to swim in. We hardly saw our father and we were mostly cared for by servants, which was fine with us.

The place looked the same now—the big house, the long stretch of driveway, the grounds—but it was set in a different light. The storm cells hadn't moved out yet, and the rain had come and gone on the drive, once coming down so hard that I couldn't see the road. There were broken branches strewn over the grounds and across the drive, and the sky was dark as smoke, lightning flashing and thunder booming as I pulled up.

The wind whipped me as I got out of the car. I had managed to buy a case of water from a variety store that was still open, so I yanked it out and climbed the front steps. I put the case down and was about to try the doorbell—it felt weird just to walk in, even in this situation—when the door was flung open and Sabrina stood there.

She was wearing yoga pants and an oversize T-shirt, and her dark hair was down. She looked so good, and I was so happy she was okay, that I didn't even think. I just scooped her up and hugged her.

There was a second of surprise, but only a second. Then she hugged me back, hard, her arms like tight bands around my neck. "Dylan!" she said.

I squeezed her harder. "Hey, Brin."

"Welcome to the party," she said against my neck. "How do you like the wedding of the year?"

I laughed. And damn it, this was the right thing to do. What had I been thinking all those years? Letting all of the shit from my childhood get to me?

I let her go, and she stood back. She lifted a fist and punched me on the shoulder, hard. "You're an asshole," she said.

"I know."

She punched me again. "Really an asshole."

"I am, Brin. I treated you like shit. I'm really sorry."

And that was all it took. Tears filled her pretty eyes and she flung herself at me again, squeezing me tight. "Asshole!" she said, this time on a sob.

I hugged her back, again, and lifted my eyes. There was a man standing in the hallway about six feet away, watching us with narrowed eyes. A big guy with dark hair whose face I'd seen in my research: Garrett Pine. He was watching over Sabrina, ready to pounce if I said the wrong thing to her.

Our eyes met. He just glared at me harder. I got the message: *Watch your step, fuckface.*

I could do that.

I let Sabrina go again just as lightning flashed and a clap of thunder sounded behind me. I picked up the case of water and brought it in. "Is everyone okay?" I asked her.

"For now," Sabrina said. "A few people left to try and brave driving. The rest of us are waiting it out here. Where's Madison?"

That brought a slice of pain right down my ribcage. I still had the image in my mind of how I'd left her, standing in the middle of our hotel room, wearing only a towel, tears tracking down her cheeks. I was hurt and I was fucking angry, but I still hated that image. I hated it a lot. "She's back at the hotel," I said.

"You should have brought her." This was a voice from the doorway. Ronnie came into the room, Clayton Rorick right behind her. Ronnie still had her wedding hair and makeup—her hair swept into an updo, her eyes dark with mascara behind her glasses, blush on her cheekbones. It was a look that clashed with the stretched-out gray Mavericks sweatshirt and old jeans she'd obviously put on when the ceremony was cancelled. But Jesus, she still looked beautiful. Ronnie had always had that cool, classic look that was hard to look away from. And she was tough and smart as hell.

I stepped forward and gave her a hug. She wasn't as enthusiastic as Brin was, but she hugged me back. When I let her go she looked up at me, frowning. "You left her at the hotel? It's safer here."

She was right. The house here was huge and sturdy. There was plenty of food and water, plus a handful of strong men for company. Garrett looked like he could handle trouble, and even though he was the tycoon type, so did Clayton. It would have been safer for Maddy here than sitting alone in a hotel with strangers.

Way to be a hero, King.

"She'll be fine," I said, hoping I sounded confident. "They'll take good care of her there."

Ronnie's eyes narrowed, and damn it, even though I hadn't seen her in years, I knew she saw right through me. "We'd take good care of her *here*," she said. "She may not be family, but she shouldn't wait out the storm alone. They say this could be the worst storm in a decade. At least we have a generator here. What if she gets hurt?"

I shook my head, and with the pain slicing through my chest, the words were out before I could think twice. "Ronnie, leave it."

Her expression tightened, and Clayton stepped right in. "Fuck you, King."

Oh, this was going well. Really, really well. Sixty seconds in the door, and Clayton was about to punch my teeth out. Then I remembered: Everyone in this room thought I was about to take over King Industries and shut out the lot of them. They thought I was walking back into their lives to send them all out of The King's Land and onto the streets.

And the hell of it was, I had almost done it. I'd been impulsive and full of my fucking ego, and I'd almost taken over an entire empire I didn't want, while permanently alienating my few family members in the process. Looking at Ronnie and Sabrina now, even with the tension in the room, it hit me like the thunderstorm outside that taking over King Industries would have been a mistake—a colossal, irreversible, life-changing mistake. To move in and make myself CEO, even with good intentions, would have ruined any chance I had of winning their trust ever again.

The only thing that had stopped me was Maddy.

Maddy with her offer. Maddy with the bonus that was now in her bank account.

"Listen," I said, returning Clayton's *fuck off* stare. "I'm here to help you guys however I can. But we have to talk about something first."

"Seems to me like there's nothing to talk about." This was

Garrett, said in his low Texas cop's drawl. "Seems to me everything's already been decided by Hank's will, hasn't it?"

"There's no time to talk now," Ronnie said. "Bea is out in the
stables helping secure the horses, and the caterers are busy
tearing the tents down. The dogs are locked up because they were
going crazy. The cell service is going in and out—I think one of
the towers has been hit. We're just trying to keep things together
until this storm passes, okay?"

"I get that, but I think we need to clear the air."

She looked at me. Ronnie had always had a backbone of steel,
even under the worst circumstances. It was how she'd resisted the
temptation of Hank's money for so many years while looking out
for her sisters. "Dylan," she said, "not now."

"Wait," I said, just as the lights blinked out. We were in
darkness.

"Shit," Garrett said. "The generator."

Outside, the rain lashed the door so hard it sounded like hail.
There was a flash of lightning, illuminating us all standing there,
and a deafening boom of thunder. The lights didn't come
back on.

"Bea is in the stables," Ronnie said.

"She should stay there," I said. The King's Land stable wasn't
the rickety structure most farmers had, of course. It was sturdy
and state of the art, made to protect very expensive horseflesh.
"She should be safe. Where's the generator?"

"Out back." I heard Clayton moving. "I'll go look at it."

"You know how to fix a generator?" This was Garrett. "Come
on, Clay. I'll fix it." There was a click, and a beam of light
appeared. "Besides, I'm the only one who has a flashlight."

"Forget it," I said. "I'll go."

"Well, for God's sake, someone go," Sabrina said. "There's
way, *way* too much testosterone in here."

23

DYLAN

THE GENERATOR WAS behind the stables, housed in a shed. Clayton, Garrett, and I had to bolt through the pouring rain from the back of the house, around the pool, and across the grounds, our way lit by Garrett's flashlight and the frequent jolts of lightning.

As soon as we approached, we could already see the problem: water was pooled at least ankle-deep around the shed.

"Shit," Garrett said over the loud wash of rain. "It's flooded."

Clayton pulled out a key and unlocked the shed while Garrett jogged off toward the stables to find equipment. When Clayton pushed open the door, we saw the generator in half a foot of water.

We were both soaked to the skin. We stood for a second, staring at the flooded shed, and then I said, "I guess we start bailing water."

I turned to find Clayton looking at me. He was the dark and handsome type, and in the moody weather he looked a little like a movie villain. I guessed Ronnie liked that type. "Listen, King," he said, his voice low with threat. "I have no idea what the hell you're playing at, but—"

"Are you seriously threatening me right now? We're a little busy here, Rorick. Though I know sitting on your ass and ordering other people around is more your thing."

"Unbelievable," he said. "You've been gone all these years, and you think you can come back and start taking over? We're going to have a discussion."

"You want a discussion?" I faced him, pushing my soaked hair back from my face. "Let's have a discussion about the two and a half mil you offered me to stay the fuck away. How did that work out for you?"

"That's over and done," he said, his jaw tight. I saw real regret in his eyes alongside the anger. "Ronnie and I have worked that out, and it's history. Something you would know if you'd even had a fucking email for Ronnie to reach you at. But you didn't. You couldn't even be bothered, because your half sisters are beneath you."

Now I was pissed. "That isn't true."

"No? Ronnie sent you an email begging you to come back after the will was read. Did you know that? But you never got it, because it bounced."

"Something you must have been happy about, since you didn't want me back anyway."

He took a step closer. "I was worried you'd hurt her."

"Me? Funny you were worried about that, since you're the one who broke her fucking heart for five years. Nice job you've done looking out for her."

"Hey," Garrett said, coming back with three shovels. "Since I'm the only one in this posse who actually owns a ranch, let me tell you that the ground isn't graded the right way here. Someone did a shit job—probably a cheap contractor Hank hired to save a few bucks. So, in order to clear this generator, we have to dig." He looked at me. "I have to be honest, Dylan. If you don't get brained with one of these shovels, it's going to be a miracle."

I took the shovel from his hand. "Oh, great. *You* have a problem with me?"

"Sabrina would have loved to have a big brother," Garrett said. "I was the one who had to defend her from the fat jokes in high school. Where were you?"

"Jesus." I turned and started to dig.

"Admit it. You've been an asshole." Garrett put his shovel in the ground, then turned to Clayton. "Though that two and a half million offer was a really low move."

"For fuck's sake," Clayton said, exasperated. "Do you really want to know why I offered that money? Because if Dylan stayed away, the estate went to me. And I was going to give all of it to Ronnie."

Garrett and I stared at him. "What did you say?" I snapped.

"I was going to give her everything. The whole estate, the money, everything. I still am. The only thing I needed"—Clayton pointed at me—"was for *you* to stay the hell away until the deadline in the will passed. But you couldn't even do that right."

"You're full of shit," I said. Because a man who would do that must really love my sister. More than anything. And the last guy I wanted to believe in was Clayton Rorick.

"It's the goddamned truth. No one asked for your opinion." Clayton put his shovel in the mud. "Keep it to yourself."

"Watch it, Clayton," Garrett said. The three of us dug for a few minutes, ankle-deep in mud as the rain soaked us. We started on a hole that would drain the water out of the shed. We were soaked and filthy, but we worked fast and the hole got bigger.

"Where is Madison, anyway?" Garrett said as he grunted and dug. "You really left her in a hotel? Sabrina said you two were serious."

"Yeah, real heroic, Superman," Clayton said as he worked.

"There's no way I'd leave Ronnie alone and unprotected in weather like this."

"No, you'd just leave her to eat or starve on her own for five years with a broken heart," I said. "You're a prince."

"He has a point," Garrett said.

Clayton stood up straight. "Really? I remember Sabrina getting kidnapped after you ripped her heart in half, Garrett. Because that was just a few days ago."

Garrett straightened and faced Clayton. "You want to take a swing at me? You want to punch the sheriff? Because I dare you to try it."

"Hey!" a woman's voice shouted. We all turned to see Bea, standing and watching us. She was wearing thick jeans and rubber boots to her knees, her slender body covered by a raincoat. Her dark hair was tied back in a practical braid and she had a silver flask in her hand that looked like it was filled with something strong.

"Bea," I said. But I didn't drop my shovel and hug her, like I'd done with Ronnie and Sabrina. She didn't look like she'd welcome it. Not that she was angry—she was just closed off.

"Dylan," she said, with a smile that was part mischief. "Nice to see you. Are you going to get this fixed?" She gestured with the flask toward the generator.

"I'm trying."

"You don't look like you're trying very hard." She raised an eyebrow as she surveyed the three of us, soaking and muddy. "None of you do. Thank God I'm done with men. I don't know what my sisters see in any of you."

"Thanks, Bea," Clayton said sarcastically.

But the three of us shut up and got to work while Bea sipped from her flask and watched. It didn't take long before water was trickling out of the generator shed into the ditch. When the water was drained, Bea walked into the shed like a royal princess in rain boots and flipped the switch. The generator sputtered and hummed to life.

"Okay, I guess you're not all bad," she said. She turned to me. "So tell me straight, Dylan. Your six months in the will are almost up. Are you taking over Dad's estate or aren't you?"

I tossed down my shovel and wiped rain from my eyes. She deserved to know—they all did. "I'm not," I told her.

Beside me, I felt Clayton Rorick go very still.

Bea stepped forward and tilted her face up, looking into my eyes. "Are you telling the truth? Because we've all been tied up in knots about this. We've been trying to reach you, but you don't make it easy."

"I know," I said. "The truth is I didn't know the terms of the will until I landed in LA a few days ago and Maddy told me. That's my fault. Hank died and I just didn't want to fucking deal with it. All those years with him hanging over my life like a dark cloud. I just wanted to be done."

Bea smiled without much humor. "I know that feeling."

"So I haven't been stringing you along on purpose. But you can ask Madison. I signed the papers. I'm out." I turned and looked at Clayton, and then I said it again. "I'm out." I raised my arms and indicated the ranch around me. "You want all of this? It's yours. Legally, the whole deal. And you didn't even have to pay me the two and a half million."

"Dylan," Clayton said.

The wind had picked up and started to howl. "It's yours," I shouted to Clayton over the sound. "Ronnie is yours, the company is yours—all of it is yours. Or hers—however you work it out. But I'm staying in the States, Rorick, and I'm not leaving. And I have some very fucking good skills. If you make a wrong move, I'll end you. I promise you that."

"You know what?" Garrett Pine said. "I've changed my mind." He pointed at me. "I like this guy. But we need to get to shelter. Now."

The stables were closer than the house, so we ducked in the heavy wind and ran there, Bea keeping up with us. We got inside the doors and I took a breath.

"I hope they're okay inside the house," Bea said.

Clayton and Garrett pushed the stable doors closed and Garrett tried to lock them. "Lock doesn't work," he muttered as both men leaned against the doors, trying to keep them from flying open in the wind. Two stable hands came over to help.

I was about to help when my cell phone rang in the back pocket of my jeans. Ronnie had said the cell service was going in and out, but still it was surprising to get a call. I pulled out my phone and saw it was Maddy.

Quickly, I answered it. "Maddy?"

"Dylan," she said. "Are you all right? I'm—"

The signal went out, the line went dead, and there was nothing more.

And then the doors flew open and the world blew apart.

24

MADDY

ONE OF THE things I've learned, after the upbringing I had, is that there are quite a few things you can accomplish with money. Sure, it can't buy happiness, but it can buy a lot of other stuff. Like, for example, a car in the middle of the worst storm in a decade.

Though technically I didn't buy the car—I rented it. The hotel owner charged me three hundred dollars, which was the cash that I had in my wallet, and I promised to bring it back.

That was how I ended up on the road to The King's Land with the rain and the wind blasting my car. I passed two cars going the other way—people taking a chance and leaving. I pressed on, hoping that no one was hurt, that I wasn't too late. Because I was of no use sitting in a dark hotel room. I could help someone.

The ranch house was dark when I pulled up, which meant the power was out here, too. I ducked through the rain and pulled open the door, calling out, "Hello? It's Madison. Is everyone okay?"

"Madison!" Ronnie's voice said. I heard her come closer, in the doorway, and I moved toward her in the dark. "You're here! Dylan said you were staying back at the hotel."

I swallowed. "Is he here?" *Is he okay?*

Ronnie took my hand and tugged me down the hallway. "He's out back, trying to fix the generator. Clayton and Garrett went with him. Frankly, the rest of us are just hoping the three of them don't kill each other."

I could see what she was worried about. Dylan and Clayton weren't exactly a mutual fan club. I had known Clayton in a professional capacity for years, and I didn't think he would take kindly to letting Dylan walk in and take over. Garrett didn't seem like the soft and squishy type, either.

Ronnie paused in the hall. Through the next doorway was the ballroom, and I could hear voices in there, people speaking softly. "We're waiting out the storm in here," Ronnie said. "This is the most central room in the house with the fewest windows. We figure that since the house doesn't have a basement, this is the safest place to be."

"I think that makes sense," I said, racking my brain for the best way to wait out a possible tornado. I'd never lived through one, so I didn't know.

But Ronnie didn't lead me into the room. Instead, she said, "Dylan came here without you. What's going on?"

Panic squeezed my rib cage. "He decided I was safer at the hotel, that's all."

"That's bullshit, Madison." The words were harsh, but her hand squeezed mine. "When I called him earlier, you were in the shower."

Oh, God. She knew. She knew.

"He said you two were a thing," Ronnie continued. "He told me it wasn't casual. That it was serious. At least to him."

He'd said that? It hurt all over again. I was glad we were in darkness because my expression would have given everything away—how I felt, how devastated I was. "Ronnie, it isn't—it isn't casual to me, either."

"Then what happened? Because something obviously did."

I forced the words out. "I kept a file on him. It was part of the job for Hank. We had investigators tracking Dylan, reporting on his movements. Taking pictures. Collecting personal information." It hurt to say it, but I did it. "He found the file. Actually, his mother paid off my assistant for it and sent it to him."

I heard Ronnie inhale. "Charlene has always been a nightmare. She's a drunk, too. Dylan has his faults, but I can't blame him for wanting to get away from her. It sounds like something she'd do."

"Yeah, well, that isn't everything she sent. She also sent him a confidential memo from my partners, congratulating me on getting him to sign the papers and forfeit the estate. And giving me a bonus for it. One I didn't ask for."

Ronnie was quiet.

I thought he must have told her; maybe he hadn't. Well, I was the estate's lawyer, and it was time to break the news. "He isn't taking the estate, Ronnie. He signed the papers. He's releasing his claim on everything."

Ronnie's voice was soft. "Why would he do that?"

"Because I told him to. I advised him." I felt my face heat. "We were getting close, and I persuaded him. But I really felt it was the right thing for him to do. I still believe that." I swallowed. "The thing is, the partners didn't tell me I'd get a bonus for getting him to sign."

"Oh, no," Ronnie said.

"He's angry. Very angry. I told him the bonus was a surprise, that it wasn't my idea, but..."

"Good lord." Ronnie sighed. "Okay, I can see that. I can see why he's upset. But he'll get over it. If he's really serious about you, he'll forgive you."

I didn't say anything. Because those were the key words, weren't they? *If he's really serious about you.* And I didn't know that. Not at all.

Even though he'd said the words to his sister, a woman he hadn't been close to in years.

Even though, in all of those old, dirty emails I shouldn't have read, he'd never once said that he was serious about another woman.

He'd said it about me. And then he'd walked away.

"I came here to help," I told Ronnie, desperate to change the subject. "Is there something I can do?"

She sighed. "I don't know. You don't happen to have a paramedic in your purse, would you?"

My heart tripped. "Why? Is someone hurt?"

"We have a little girl here, Julia. She's ten. She has asthma. The dark and the storm are frightening her and making it worse. She's with her mother, and she has an inhaler, but she probably shouldn't be here. She's starting to panic. What if she has a full-out attack?"

"I'll take them," I said. "You're right, she should probably be in a hospital for observation, just in case. How far is the nearest hospital?"

"It's probably forty-five minutes. Faster if you speed."

I felt my spine stiffen with resolve. "I can do it, but we need to leave now. Right now. It's still driveable out there, but maybe not for long." I could feel Ronnie hesitate. "Ronnie, if we don't leave now, it could be hours before we can go. And if there are trees or power lines down over the roads after this storm, it could be even longer. Paramedics are going to be overwhelmed as it is."

"Okay," Ronnie said. "You're right. Okay. Take them. But be quick. And for God's sake, be safe."

THE FIRST TWENTY minutes went just fine. Both Julia and her mother sat in the back seat of my sort-of-rented car while I drove as fast as I safely could. Julia's mother's name was Jenny, and she sat with her arms around her daughter, inhaler at the ready as Julia sat quietly and tried not to cry.

The sky got darker and the wind felt like it might actually tilt the car. I'd never felt anything like it. *Don't panic, Maddy. Don't panic.*

But Julia wasn't fooled. "Are we going to make it?" she asked.

"We aren't going to make it."

"Hush, sweetie," Jenny said, rubbing her daughter's arms. "We'll be just fine, don't you worry."

But Julia twisted away from her mother and looked out the back window. "Mom, look! It's a tornado!"

I glanced in my rearview mirror and nearly drove off the road. There was a funnel cloud a few miles behind us. It was pitch black and huge, and the way it moved looked strangely alive, as if it was somehow sentient. I'd never seen anything so terrifying, and so weirdly almost beautiful, in my life.

And it was behind us. At The King's Land.

There was a tornado at The King's Land.

I couldn't scream. I couldn't panic. I had a little girl in the car with me who was already on the verge of an asthma attack. I forced myself to look away from the rearview and keep driving, edging the gas a little harder. There weren't even any houses or other structures along this stretch of road, nowhere to pull over and hide. I had no idea what I was supposed to do, but *keep driving and get the hell away from the tornado* seemed like a good bet.

"Go faster, Maddy," Jenny said. She, too, was fighting to keep calm, but I could hear the panic in her voice.

"I'm on it," I said.

And I thought it might be fine. There was no one else on the road, at least until we got to the main highway. There might be traffic there. But if I could take back roads to get to the hospital, maybe we could—

Dylan, I thought. *Take cover, Dylan. Please. Please.*

Panic tried to rise in my throat again. Ronnie, Sabrina, Bea, Clayton, Garrett...they were all still there. The house was big and sturdy and they were all probably fine. But probably wasn't good enough. That tornado was *terrifying.*

Please be okay, Dylan. Please.

The wind blasted the car again under flashes of lightning, and the thought crossed my mind that the people I'd left in the house might be safer than we were, tornado or no tornado. Couldn't tornadoes flip cars? Or had I only seen that in movies? Jesus, law school didn't prepare you for this kind of thing.

If we could just get to the hospital. It was a little bit farther—

Julia screamed.

Something was coming at us. A dark shadow that formed into a tree branch—a huge one, heading for the windshield. I turned the wheel to try and avoid it and felt the back tires slip on the gravel at the side of the road. Then the branch hit the car with a sickening *crack.* Julia and Jenny screamed, and the car spun off the road into the ditch.

For a second there was silence except for the pounding of rain and the screaming of the wind. My shoulder ached where the seatbelt had cut into it, my jaw ached, and I was sitting tilted at an angle with the branch on the windshield in front of my face, but otherwise I was alive. "Is everyone okay?" I called out, unbuckling my seatbelt and trying to turn in my seat.

"We're all right, I think," Jenny said. I could hear Julia's heavy breathing. I turned and saw them both in the back seat, tilted at the same crazy angle, Jenny's arms around Julia. "Maybe we should—"

There was another crash, and we all screamed—me, too, this

time. Something big and heavy hit the car. I looked out the window to see it was a shed—literally someone's garden shed, picked up from God knew how far away and flung by the wind. Now it sat lodged against our tilted car, wedged into the passenger-side door. The driver's side, I realized, was flush against the dirt and grass of the ditch, which meant we couldn't get out.

There was a thin wheezing sound from the back. I turned back to see Jenny putting the inhaler to her daughter's mouth. Julia was pale and still, her eyes wide with panic, her chest moving as she fought to breathe.

"It's okay, sweetie," Jenny said softly. "Just breathe. We're all safe. It's okay."

I reached back and took Julia's hand, holding it and stroking it. It was ice cold. Jesus, how had this happened? I'd woken up this morning in my condo in LA, packing to go to the airport to go to the wedding of the year. And now, here I was.

I dug out my cell phone and saw, miraculously, that it had a single bar. I dialed Dylan.

He answered almost immediately, and I almost wept to hear his voice. "Maddy?"

"Dylan, are you all right? I'm in a car by the side of the road. Highway 2, I think. I crashed into a ditch, but we're all okay. Where are you?"

But there was nothing on the other end. The signal was dead.

I put the phone down and squeezed Julia's cold hand as she breathed in, out, in again. "It's okay," I told her softly, adding my voice to her mother's. "We're going to wait it out here. The storm's going to pass over us, and then we'll get out and go to the hospital. Just hold on, honey. Breathe and hold on."

I listened to the thin sound of her breathing, the soft sound of Jenny talking to her daughter, and hoped to hell I was right. Hoped that Dylan had heard me. Hoped that something, anything, would get us out of here.

25

DYLAN

LATER, I wondered how long the whole thing took. Ten minutes? Twenty? In some ways it felt like seconds, and in other ways it felt like a year.

The King's Land stables, fortunately, were built like a fortress. Hank's prized horses were worth a lot of money, and he valued them more than he valued most of the people he met. So we sheltered in the overhang beneath the loft as the tornado blasted through and the horses kicked up a fuss in their stalls. Luckily Bea and the stable hands had bedded the horses down properly, including hoods over their eyes, so they wouldn't panic and hurt themselves. We heard something smash against the outside of the stable, and a ripping noise that was probably shingles coming off the roof. A disembodied fence hurtled past the doorway and disappeared. The sound was almost deafening.

And then it stopped.

We looked at each other for a long minute after the silence

fell. The light was still dark and yellowish purple, the wind was still whistling, but the waterfall-like roar was gone. The tornado had moved on. Bea, Garrett, Clayton, and I all exchanged a look, all of us thinking the same thing.

"The house," Bea said.

We stood and sprinted out of the stables toward the house. There was debris everywhere: shingles, broken fences, heavy branches, planks of wood. The shed around the generator was demolished, though the generator itself was still in place. I could see broken windows on the ranch house, and one of the back doors was ripped off. *Please let everyone be okay.*

Maddy. Where is Maddy?

I was going to make sure everyone in the house was all right. And then I was going to fucking find her.

"Ronnie!" Clayton tore through the broken back door, past the soaked entry hall and into the ballroom. The lights were out again—so much for all of our work digging.

Ronnie came from the dark ballroom and threw herself into Clayton's arms. Sabrina was right behind her, launching herself at Garrett. It was touching—even Bea looked moved. I brushed past everyone and checked the ballroom, where everyone had waited out the tornado. The house had held, and everyone was fine.

I left the ballroom and strode toward the front door. I heard footsteps behind me. "Dylan! Where are you going?"

It was Ronnie. "I'm going back to the hotel," I told her. "Maddy called me. I have to get her."

"She called you?" Ronnie put a hand on my arm to stop me. "Dylan, she's not at the hotel. She came here. She took one of the guests and her daughter to the hospital. The daughter has asthma and was starting to panic. When did she call you?"

"Right before the tornado hit." I scrubbed a hand through my hair. Jesus—Maddy had been on the road, unprotected, trying to help. What a fucking fool I'd been, leaving her alone. "The signal cut out, but I heard her voice. Tell me where she went—the exact route."

Ronnie looked pale. "Maybe she's fine. Maybe they made it and she was just calling to check on you."

I looked at her. We both knew the odds were that wasn't the truth. I felt it in my gut, a screaming instinct that something was wrong. That with every minute that ticked by, it was going to go more and more wrong.

"Tell me the route," I said to her again.

"At least take Garrett with you. He's the sheriff. If someone needs help, maybe he can help them."

"Ronnie. Tell me where she went."

She bit her lip, and then she told me. What roads were the shortest route to the hospital—the way Maddy would have taken. I thanked her, gave her a quick kiss on the cheek, and took off for my car.

I tried dialing Maddy's number over and over, but the signal was out. I pulled onto the road, avoiding the debris and fallen branches that strewed the driveway, and followed Maddy's trail. In my rearview mirror, I saw a big SUV pull out of the driveway behind me—Garrett, probably. I wasn't going to shake him, and that was fine with me. If he wanted to follow and help me out, I could use it.

It took us nearly an hour, picking our way down first one road and then another. We had to weave through the debris, and three times we had to stop entirely and haul tree branches from the road. We had to drive on the shoulder at one point to avoid fallen power lines. There were a few cars out, people trying to collect their loved ones or start the cleanup. I still dialed Maddy's phone over and over, but the cell towers must have been damaged, because nothing went through.

The longer it took, the more I panicked. She was hurt some-where—I didn't know how I knew it, but I knew it. With every minute that spun out, I could feel her getting farther from me. If she was in pain, or unconscious, the clock was ticking. I *needed* to find her.

I was soaked and filthy from the storm, and in the hot, close air that followed as the storm cells broke up I felt sweat coating my back. Garrett worked tirelessly alongside me, helping move debris off the road, reassuring people that he was the sheriff and everything would be fine. His dress pants and button-down shirt, which were the remnants of his wedding-guest clothes, were completely ruined, his dress shoes were coated in mud, and he was as soaked in sweat as I was. Still, we followed Maddy's route, searching.

"What the hell is that?" Garrett had pulled up beside me in his SUV as we made our way down the two-lane blacktop, our windows rolled down so we could shout at each other. I followed where he was pointing and saw a garden shed lying in a ditch. There was something beneath it.

When I got closer, I saw it was a car, crashed into the ditch, the doors pinned shut by its angle to the ground and the shed on top of it.

I'd never seen that car before.

Maddy, all my instincts said.

I stopped the car in the middle of the road and got out, not bothering to close the door behind me. I splashed into the muddy ditch and approached the car. "There's someone inside!" I shouted up at Garrett. "I can hear voices!"

Someone was shouting inside the car; a fist knocked on a window. Garrett and I got into position and pushed on the shed, trying to haul it off. It wouldn't move.

"Again!" Garrett shouted.

We pushed again, sweating and straining, and I quietly thanked Providence that I'd started this mission with a former football quarterback who was probably the strongest guy at The King's Land. We pushed again, and again, while people shouted inside the car and the hot post-storm sun beat down on our backs.

Finally, the shed budged. We rocked it back and forth, then tilted it and slid it off the car. The passenger door was buckled, but I yanked it hard and it finally opened.

Maddy was there.

She was pale, disheveled, sweaty, and she had a bruise on her forehead. She had tear stains on her cheeks. But it was Maddy. All of her, alive and whole and breathing. I pulled her up and into my arms and she wrapped herself around me, sobbing. I held her like I'd never let her go.

Over her shoulder, I watched Garrett pull a woman and a young girl out of the car, the girl with an inhaler in her hand. "Are you okay?" I said to Maddy. "Are you hurt?"

"No," she said, not loosening her grip on me. "I'm bruised, but nothing's broken. I'm so happy to see you." Her voice broke on the last word.

"I'm so sorry," I said against her neck, inhaling the warm scent of her skin. "Maddy, I am so fucking sorry." God, what if something had happened to her? I'd spend the rest of my life feeling nothing but sorry. I had come so close.

"I'm sorry, too," she said. "I should have told you about the file. I'll give the bonus back and—"

"Forget it," I said. "It doesn't matter." I loosened my grip and looked at her face, cradling her jaw gently in my hands. "Nothing matters except that you're okay." I kissed her, long and hard, and she kissed me back, her arms winding around my neck, her hands going into my hair.

When she broke the kiss she said, "We couldn't get out of there. We couldn't call anyone. If you hadn't gotten here..." She stopped, like the words wouldn't come.

I stroked her back. "Of course I came for you," I said. "I'd come for you anywhere. I'd never fucking stop until I found you. Do you understand?"

She nodded, though she didn't seem inclined to let me go. "Is everyone at the ranch okay?"

"Everyone is fine. Medieval kings had nothing on Hank. That place could probably withstand an army."

That got me a smile, though it was a weak one. "We should get Julia to a hospital."

That must be the little girl. I could see that Garrett had already loaded her and her mother into his SUV. "Garrett will take them. You need to get in the car with me."

"Where are we going?"

I kissed her again, briefly. "You need food and water. We both need a bath. And then I think that as soon as the flights are going again, we should get the hell out of Texas."

Her dark brown eyes looked into mine, and I saw everything I wanted there. Beauty and brains and humor and toughness and a sweet, buried vulnerability. And sexiness. And, maybe—I hoped—love.

"You really are a superhero," she said with a smile.

I leaned in and kissed her. "If you think so, then I'll do my best," I said. "Let's go."

26

MADDY

IT WASN'T the wedding of the century, but it was a wedding.

My wedding.

The one thing I'd never thought would happen was actually happening: I was getting married. To Dylan King.

It was six months after the day of the tornado, and the LA sky was dark and dreary. It was two weeks until Christmas, which was the strangest time in California: lights and Christmas trees and presents under cool skies, smog, and palm trees. It was very weird, and I loved it.

I stood in front of the mirror and straightened my dress. It didn't look much like a wedding gown, which was the way I wanted it. It was a simple knee-length dress of dark gray with a deep V neck and a slim belt at the waist. I had my hair brushed down my back and tied back at the temples, simple makeup, a few pieces of jewelry, and heels. I felt...beautiful.

Because I felt like myself. I was a woman who worked hard

and made money and liked to look nice, but I wasn't a woman who needed to prove anything to anyone. I was also a woman getting married to the man she was deeply, crazily in love with.

The last six months had been better than I'd ever thought possible. Not because they'd been particularly eventful—though they felt eventful to me. I'd gone back to work and lived my life, but piece by piece, I'd become a different woman. I'd felt so much change within myself that I wondered why the rest of the world wasn't as breathless as I was, trying to keep up.

While Ronnie and Sabrina had stayed in Texas—and had invited us countless times to come live there—Dylan and I had stayed in LA. We both liked it here, and more importantly, both of our careers were here. I worked best from the firm's LA office, where I could closely oversee all of the employees and the client accounts. Dylan, now that he wasn't going to be CEO of King Industries, had partnered with his friend and former Special Ops colleague, Eli McLean, in his private security business. They took contracts that Dylan sometimes couldn't talk about, but that paid insane amounts of money. Because apparently—and this was no surprise to me—they were very, very good.

Clayton had taken over King Industries, except he'd given up one thing—Hank's LA condo. He'd given that as a gift to Dylan and me, accompanied by the simple sentiment: *No hard feelings.* Even without the gift of the condo, there were none—Clayton was doing an incredible job leading Hank's company and managing his legacy. But I had sold my own condo and Dylan and I had moved in, redecorating and making the place our own.

I'd never lived with a boyfriend before, and Dylan had spent over a decade on military bases, so we shouldn't have worked. But we did—we really did. We liked the same food and the same kinds of wine. I hated clutter, and Dylan only owned a bag's worth of belongings. He gave me most of the closet without a fight. I bought him clothes, because it was fun to buy things to put on his sexy body. He got up half an hour earlier than I did on weekends and brought me a fancy coffee from the coffee shop, because he knew it made me happy. Which it did every time.

He was intelligent and funny and brilliant and gorgeous, and the sex...dear God, the sex. There was a lot of it, and it was incredible. We wore each other out regularly, and then we rested and did it again. To be honest, although I was still working hard, I wasn't working *quite* as many hours as I used to. Or I was taking more work home. Because at home was Dylan and all that sex.

He'd proposed to me in bed, in fact. With his body cradling mine and his muscled arm around me and his face buried in my neck. *Marry me,* he'd said. *Just marry me.* A proposal that was simple and straightforward and went straight to my heart, like Dylan himself.

I'd said yes. And now here we were.

We'd thought about doing City Hall, but when Sabrina got wind of that, she wouldn't hear of it. We refused to do a big wedding—that seemed to be a curse in the King family—but we had to do *something.* Brin's argument was that the entire King family had been deprived of a wedding when the tornado blew Ronnie's away. The fact that she was marrying Garrett Pine, and the wedding was undoubtedly going to be An Event, didn't count. Her one and only brother couldn't get married without some kind of party to mark the occasion.

So we'd compromised. We'd rented a small hall and brought in a justice of the peace. The catering was simple and the alcohol would be champagne. We invited a dozen close friends, family, and clients. And as soon as I was ready, I'd go out and get married.

I looked at myself in the mirror and thought about the scared girl who'd had an anxiety attack when the cops came to break up her parents' fight. That girl was still there, but she wasn't quite as afraid anymore. She thought that maybe her past was behind her.

Behind me, the door opened and I saw the familiar figure of my husband-to-be, dressed in one of his gorgeous suits that pretty much made my panties drop. Just like he did no matter what he was wearing.

"You're not supposed to be here," I said, turning from the mirror.

"I know," he said, coming toward me. "I couldn't resist." He looked as gorgeous as ever, with his dark hair worn just a little long, his beard trim against his jaw. He'd offered to shave it if I wanted, but I said no. I liked the feel of it on my inner thighs—a fact I didn't admit aloud to him for fear of how big it would expand his ego.

When he came close I put my palms on his lapels, smoothing them. Oh, he even smelled good. Divine. "You look very handsome," I admitted.

"I know," he said again. He gently put his fingertips to my hips and lifted my skirt. An inch. Two. "You look beautiful, Mrs. King," he said, smiling down at me.

"We're not married yet," I protested, trying to focus as his fingertips hitched my skirt a little higher. "And I'm not Mrs. King." I wasn't going to change my name—we'd already decided that. Again, Dylan's ego. "But I'll take the compliment."

"Will you?" He hitched my skirt high enough to get his hands beneath it, and he traced his fingertips along my thighs. "That's very kind of you, Mrs. King." He bent and kissed the side of my neck. The spot I liked best—the spot that made me wet for him every time he kissed me there.

"What are you doing?" I asked, my voice a little strangled as his fingertips continued their exploration.

"Checking that you're certain you want to marry me," he said against my skin, kissing me again. "Speak now or forever hold your peace, Maddy."

Was he insane? Of course I wanted to marry him. Did he think I was going to say *no thanks?* The little girl I'd been woke up at night sometimes, worrying that it would be him who backed out. That it would be Dylan who decided that my shit was too much to deal with, that all of this was too hard, and he had some-where else to be.

But he hadn't done that. And neither had I.

I put my hands on his shoulders, stroking them and enjoying the feel through the fabric of his suit. "I'll marry you," I said, keeping my voice light. "You have certain qualities that I suppose I can put up with."

"Such as?" His fingers found my pussy through my panties, stroked it gently.

"If I tell you, it will just feed your ego."

I felt him smile against my skin, and his fingers didn't stop moving, thank God. I was starting to feel boneless.

"I suppose I should ask you the same question," I said, trying to keep my voice from shaking. God, I loved the way he touched me. He was so perfect at it, like he knew everything I wanted before I did. "Since we're here and all of our guests are outside, waiting for us to get married. Are you sure you want to be tied to only one woman for the rest of your life?"

He kissed my neck softly. He was avoiding kissing my mouth, I knew, because I had just done my nice wedding makeup and he didn't want to ruin it. That was the kind of thing Dylan picked up on, like he was psychic. "Depends on the woman," he said. "If the woman is you, then yes, I'm fine with it."

He would not make me melt. No way. Not now. "Think it over. You have quite a history, Mr. King."

A history I'd seen pictures of. Though the infamous file was long gone, deleted into the digital ether. But still.

"I do have quite a history," Dylan agreed. His fingers pushed my panties aside and moved inside them, making me hiss in a breath. "Let's see. There was the time we went to Sonoma for the weekend and did it in the hot tub. And the time I bent you over the kitchen counter when you came home from work. Oh, wait, that was more than once." He was rubbing my pussy now, in the perfect way he always did it, and I should probably have stopped him, but the thought never crossed my mind. Instead I panted and pressed my legs open to give him better access. Because Dylan made me weak, he always had, and that was just fine with me.

"Then," he continued as he pleasured me, "there was the time I woke up and you already had your mouth on me. That time was particularly dirty. Or the time I took you out to dinner and found out halfway through the meal that you had no panties on under your skirt."

I tilted my head back as pleasure swirled through me. It was good. It was so, so good, and just the sound of his voice made it better.

"So, yes," Dylan said, leaning in to kiss my neck again, "you could say I have quite a history. With you. That's why I plan to marry you. Just as soon as I make you come."

I gripped his lapels as pleasure pulsed through me. "God, you're about to," I breathed.

"Let me see it," he said in my ear, and I came on his fingers, my body shaking and flushing hot, my hips pressing down on him. I bit my lip to keep from shouting. He put an arm around my waist to keep me upright.

It took me a minute or two to come down, and then I sighed. I really was literally swooning. "I love you, Dylan," I said.

That made him smile. It wasn't one of his cocky smiles—it was a real one, laced with delight and a little bit of surprise. I was the only person Dylan gave that particular smile to, and it always stopped my heart when I saw it. It was the smile that said how he felt about me. Truly.

"I love you, too," Dylan King said. "Let's go get married."

A NOTE FROM THE AUTHORS

Thank you for reading the King Family series! We hope you enjoyed it.

If you missed the other books, they are:

The Tycoon by M. O'Keefe (Book 1)

The Bodyguard by S. Doyle (Book 2)

Yes, Bea is getting a book! It's called The Cowboy, it's by M. O'Keefe, and it's coming in Fall 2018!

ALSO BY JULIE KRISS

The Riggs Brothers Series

Drive Me Wild

Take Me Down

Work Me Up

The Bad Billionaire Series

Bad Billionaire

Dirty Sweet Wild

Rich Dirty Dangerous

Back in Black

Standalone

Spite Club

The Eden Hills Duet

Bad Boyfriend

Bad Wedding

Made in the USA
Las Vegas, NV
12 February 2021

17678790R00111